PSYCHIC

GAMES

I0625141

Kate Allenton

Published by Coastal Escape Publishing

Discover other titles by Kate Allenton

At http://www.kateallenton.com

PSYCHIC GAMES

DEDICATION

For my Mother-In-Law, Gayle who lost her
battle with ovarian cancer.

May you rest in peace.

ACKNOWLEDGMENTS

This book would not be in existence without the love and support of my family and friends who gave me the gentle nudge needed to see this through. Thank you. I appreciate each and every one of you

Chapter 1

Grace bounced her crossed leg as she flipped impatiently through a magazine in the dating agency office. Why was she here? As a favor, of course. Why else would anyone wait thirty minutes beyond an appointment time just to be matched with some losers? She had a job she loved, a family that loved her back, and she could get any man she set her mind on. She needed a dating agency service much like she needed to rub honey all over her body and stand atop an anthill. Neither promised a good time. And yet, here she sat with a room full of women looking for love. They'd have better chances by calling Linked Inc. At least the psychics that worked for her would be more accurate. Maybe she should leave some business cards near the magazines.

The clock ticking on the wall grated on her nerves and taunted the precious time she'd never get back. The unease in the room was thick and choking. The only person speaking was the receptionist, who was on a personal call. Unprofessional, check, check. And this company claimed to have a ninety-eight percent success rate in the first match. What a load of...

The door across the room opened, cutting off Grace's thought. A woman in her sixties wearing a polyester suit, and her hair up in a tight bun, gave Grace a pinched smile. "Ms. Thornton?"

Finally. Grace tossed the magazine aside and grabbed her purse. If she'd been forced to wait another ten minutes she'd have to go back to her best friend, Chloe, without any answers. Grace followed behind the lady while fighting the nerves in her stomach to keep it from flipping. She could do this. She was undercover. A female version of James Bond. Maybe she should have brought her Taser. That might have made the wait more entertaining.

The woman stopped and gestured to an office. "If you'll take a seat, Mr. Stone will be in shortly. He's just finishing up his meeting."

Grace walked into the room and turned to thank the lady, only to find that the door was already closed and the woman had vanished ninja-style, leaving Grace alone in the big corner office. If that woman worked for Grace, she'd buy her a pair of squeaky shoes and a bell for Christmas, and probably be reported to HR for targeting seniors.

Expensive cologne teased her nose. The dark cherry wood and leather furnishings made the room feel like her father's home office. She should have sat as she'd been instructed. She never did follow instructions.

Grace walked around the room, running her finger over the polished bookshelf. Not a dust speck in sight. She moved to the pictures on the wall. Several diplomas and awards were displayed for the infamous Sam Stone. The guy was book smart to her street smart. They were going to get along like peanut butter and spinach.

She walked to the desk. Neat and tidy. Nothing for her to even snoop through. This guy was boring, but the view was fantastic. Grace stood in front of the window and glanced over at Linked Inc.'s building. Her office sat directly facing his. Her blinds were open; the room was dark.

This would be the perfect place to spy on her sisters. If she still did that kind of thing.

"Do you like the view?"

She swiveled around to find tall, dark, and yummy in a black Armani suit standing in the room. The enemy. A smile split her lips as she let her gaze travel down his body and back up, making him feel as ridiculous as she did for even agreeing to this cockamamie scheme. "I do now."

His lips twitched as he closed the door behind him. "One of the Thornton five. I never thought I'd see the day."

Ohh. He'd heard of her. Score one point for him. She was totally keeping tally.

"I see you've done your research, Mr. Stone."

"I like to know my neighbors."

"Tell me, what else do you know?" she asked, moving back around the desk to sit in one of the chairs, crossing her legs seductively. A total Sharon Stone move. His gaze followed the movement. So, he wasn't gay like Chloe had heard through the grape vine. Score one for Grace. She could work with that.

"I take my job seriously, Ms. Thornton, and I must admit you checked all the right boxes on the application, although you'll have to forgive me for not taking you at your word. Successful, beautiful, you're not in a relationship, and you're a medium. I think that sums it up."

"Sharp-tongued, smartass, hates animals. Which part bothers you most?"

"We aren't here to discuss me." He cleared his throat and took his seat. He leaned back in his chair, the leather creaking under his weight, and steepled his fingers. His gaze never left hers. The move was one she'd expect from a principal or therapist. If her principal had been as good looking as this enemy, she might have skipped more and been one of the perpetual problem kids. She wouldn't have minded sitting in his office all day. "What I'd like to know is, why are you here?"

"To find Mr. Right." She smiled brightly. The answer came as quickly as she'd rehearsed. "Isn't that why everyone comes here?"

"You don't strike me as the kind of woman who needs my services. We serve three categories of women. The shy ones who have a hard time meeting someone. The kind that is tired of falling for the wrong men, and the ones looking for a rebound without putting in the effort of finding a match for themselves. You don't fit into one of those boxes. So, let's be honest here. I can't help you unless I know what I'm up against. Why is it you can't find Mr. Right?"

His arrogance floated around the room in a cloud of haze, much like the pot haze in her college apartment when her friends came over to have a good time. She hadn't inhaled then, but she would now. He had a right to be arrogant. She didn't fit neatly into any of his bland brown boxes, as he'd suggested, because she was a 100 percent fraud, much like the politicians running for office.

Make something up. Chloe's voice echoed in Grace's head, reminding her why she'd come. What would be the one reason that would push Mr. Arrogance's buttons? "He doesn't exist."

Stew on that. Grace rose from her chair, walked over to his window, and pointed down to the street below at the people walking by. "I've met my share of men. Some were nice, cordial, and some even made me feel special, but I want more than that. I want something that I haven't found on my own. Something that I've searched long and hard for." She glanced at him to find he'd risen from his seat. "The kind of man I want simply doesn't exist."

"What was missing?" he asked, crossing his arms over his chest as he moved to stand beside her.

"The pitter-patter of my heart when he enters the room. Butterflies doing somersaults in my stomach. The heat from his gaze. The longing for his touch. I crave desire, love, and honesty."

Even now her body trembled just saying the words out loud, as though it was therapeutic. Heat scoured her cheeks. One look at her and he'd believe her words. She'd meant them. "Do you have anyone in your databank that would fit my needs?"

****

She was good. He'd give her that. But he knew her game. It was a challenge. Giving him a list of qualities that he'd never be able to fill. What she didn't know about was the private investigation that went into each applicant. He was aware that she was beautiful and smart and her best friend was his competition. Heck, he even knew how she liked her coffee. What she was asking for was chemistry, and not something he could find in one of his client's profiles. Time to make her squirm. Turnabout was fair play, after all.

"Do you have anything against sex?"

She turned to look at him and smiled. "I like sex just fine."

"If we take you as a client, you'll be asked to abstain on your dates for the time being."

"That shouldn't be a problem." She turned and crossed her arms beneath her breasts, pushing them up in the little sheer camisole she was wearing. That was a classic move, much like the way she'd seductively crossed her legs. He kept his gaze on hers, ignoring the baser need to check her rack. "I don't need a man's touch to find release."

She'd said the comment with barely a blush. What he wouldn't do to see exactly what it would take to make her turn the color of a ripe tomato.

"What about bondage? Anything we should know? There's no sense on pairing you with a vanilla lover if you're more the experimental type. We like to nail our matches right out of the gate. We make them last that way."

Her mouth parted before she quickly snapped it shut and licked her lips. The idea intrigued her. He could read it in her eyes.

"I'd like to think I'm pretty adventurous in bed. I'll try anything once."

Damn her. He'd expected her to gawk and get flustered. Yet she held his gaze, challenging him to produce someone who would fit the bill.

"Tall, dark hair, successful. Secure enough within himself to date an attractive, successful woman. Good in bed, passionate, romantic, muscular body, and smart. He'd have to be able to keep up with you. Does that about describe the type of guy you're looking for?"

"You left out adventurous and open-minded. He'd have to be able to put up with my career choice."

He moistened his lips as he took in the desire shining in her eyes. That was exactly what she wanted. No wonder no man had given her what she needed. They'd never taken the time to read her eyes. They told him everything without her even opening her red, kissable lips.

"And if I find you a guy who fits every one of those aspects, you'll agree to the three-date clause in your contract?"

"Are you saying you can find me someone?"

"I'm saying I'll try my best, but only after I really get to know you can I know what type of guy is going to make you tick."

"I thought we just went over that."

"We did. But I need the big picture of how you are around men that are interested in you. Your body language, the attitude you give off, everything, if I'm going to find Mr. Right and not just Mr. Right now." He sat back down in his chair, pulled out her file, and flipped it open. "We need a week of your time. Can you take time off?"

"A full week?"

"Yes." He signed his name on the contract, turned it to face her, and held out his pen. "An entire week should give us more of an idea of who you are and what type of man would make you happy."

Hesitation flickered in her eyes.

"Those are my terms."

She slipped the pen out of his hand and nibbled her bottom lip between her teeth as she signed. Tossing the pen onto his desk, she picked up her purse and headed for the door. "You've got one full week to get me figured out."

"I'll send the limo to pick you up at seven. Pack a bag with a few casual outfits and a nice dress or two."

"Wait." She spun around. "You didn't say anything about leaving town."

"There's no need to worry, Ms. Thornton. You'll be accompanying me, so you'll be completely safe and never in a compromising situation."

"I'm spending the week with you? That doesn't seem very professional. Are you sure you aren't using your dating company for your own hook-ups?" She teased.

"Do I look like a man that needs to use my company to find women? You're asking me to perform the impossible. I have to go out of town, and I'd like to get started with you right away. I have a feeling I've got my work cut out for me. A week with me is small in comparison to the potential prize. Don't you agree?"

Chapter 2

Grace dialed her best friend and slipped the Bluetooth in her ear as she crossed the street.

"How did it go?" Chloe's voice vibrated in excitement.

"You're going to owe me big time."

"I already do. So, don't keep me in suspense. How was he?"

"Horrible. Arrogant, smart like Yoda, and cunning like Vader. Beautiful and not gay."

"Did he say, Grace, I am your father?" Chloe asked in her best Vader voice, complete with loud breaths, before she chuckled.

"No, but if he'd said, come to daddy, I would have jumped on that train and pulled the whistle."

"Oh, whoever he is, he sounds like fun." Grace's sister, Quinn, said walking up beside her as they both entered the building.

Grace slid her card key through the security panel to call the elevator. "Chloe, I'll have to call you back. Quinn decided to live vicariously through me now that she's married."

"Lunch at eleven at Luigi's?"

"Sounds fabulous." Grace clicked her Bluetooth off.

"So who's daddy and how big is his whistle?" Quinn asked, holding her round belly. She'd been married less than a year, and she was about to drop any day.

The elevator opened on their floor, saving Grace from having to explain. "Don't you have a Highlander waiting at your house? Why are you here?"

"Ian is showing Collin the new house he bought and then meeting me here. Besides, I wouldn't have missed this for the world."

"Missed what?" Grace asked, turning into her office. She paused in her tracks. Her sisters were sitting in the dark. Binoculars lined the desk. Her sisters had converged like a pack of virgins waiting for a first-hand account of the man's snickerdoodle.

Grace flicked on her office light.

"Honey, if you needed a date, Cooper could have introduced you to a few of his friends," Cara said, holding her belly while rising from Grace's desk chair.

"Who had the vision?" Grace asked, sliding around her sisters who were crowding her office.

"Aunt Betty," they all said at once.

"What did she see? What's the verdict?"

Cara shared a look with Quinn and Harper with Becca. Grace could have heard a fairy's wings flutter in the silence.

"Spill it," Grace growled, placing a balled fist on her hip.

"Whatever you're going to do, you need to cancel." Cara clasped her fingers together in front of her.

"And never see him again," Harper added.

"Ever," Becca concurred.

This was the first time in her entire life the sisters had agreed, and with an amount of conviction that startled Grace. Would the sky fall? Would the heavens open and swallow them up whole? It couldn't be that bad, right? "What about you, Quinn?"

Quinn had always been the more outspoken of Grace's sister. She'd give her opinion whether the person wanted it or not. She'd been the reigning mayor of crazy town. If Quinn agreed with the others, that alone would have her second-guessing the arrangement.

"How hot was he?" Quinn asked, earning her a smack on the arm from Harper. "Oww."

Grace lifted her brow and fought back the smile from her lips.

"Fine. I agree. There's no way you'll come out smelling like roses with Mr. Douche's shady past. No matter how many times you partake in his supersized extra-large Italian sausage."

Grace collapsed into her chair. "Well, crap."

"Don't worry, dear. We'll take care of everything," Cara announced as she left the room with her sisters in tow.

"Wait, what?" It took a minute for Cara's words to register. Grace hurried around her desk to see her sisters getting on the elevator. She ran to stop them.

"Don't worry." Quinn had said those same famous last words the day three feet of detergent and bubbles covered the laundry room floor when she'd been teaching Grace how to clean dishes quicker in the washing machine.

The elevator doors slid closed in Grace's face.

Oh, the horror. A shiver skirted down Grace's spine. With her luck, she'd end up married to the man, instead of out of the contract, when her sisters were done. Grace hurried back into her office and killed the lights. She grabbed a pair of the binoculars and glanced down at the street below where her sisters were crossing and headed straight toward the dating agency building.

"This isn't happening." She lifted the binoculars to Stone's window, and her heartbeat sped. He was standing at his office window staring directly at hers. Could he feel the disturbance in the Force?

Grace didn't lower the binoculars, and she didn't hide behind the wall. He couldn't have paid her to look away from the tornado that was about to blow into his office. No way would her sisters be corralled in the waiting room. If Grace could only read lips. James Bond would have hidden a bug to listen in. Damn her spy skills.

The office door burst open behind him. Ninja lady was walking backward with her hands held out.

"Poor, poor woman. I'm going to have to send her a crate of wine to help her forget meeting my sisters."

****

Sam watched in amusement as the rest of the Thatcher sisters waited for Grace to return. Their surprise attack when Grace flipped on the light made him chuckle. He'd stood at the window waiting to see if Grace would be like the rest and pick up a pair of binoculars. He hadn't had to wait long, just long enough for the rest of them to leave for her to give in. Only her gaze wasn't on him. He followed the direction of the binoculars to find the rest of the Thatcher women crossing the street. He should have known nothing would be easy with Grace. He met her gaze once more before his door opened and Iris was pleading with them to make an appointment. He spun around.

"It's okay, Iris."

Iris gave him a worried look, and he gave her a nod. He hadn't even waited until the door was shut before he spoke. "All of the Thatcher Five in one day. I'm sure none of you married ladies are here for my services, so I assume this is either a social visit or you wanted to see if I'd give you a discount for signing Becca, your only other single sister."

The redhead, Quinn, pushed through the crowd with her big belly leading the way. Two of the women looked ready to go into labor. "We're here to tell you to back off of our sister."

"Is that right?" Sam asked and retook his seat.

"Hi, I'm Cara, and what Quinn meant was that Grace will no longer be needing your services, so whatever dates you may have arranged, you'll have to cancel," the blonde announced.

"I know all of your names."

"Well, that's great. We'll be glad to pay out the remainder of her contract and reimburse you for your time," Harper said.

He watched them all work in tandem. When one quit talking, the next started. When one offended, the other corrected. They were an interesting bunch, and yet all of them were dead set against Grace working with him. The question was why?

"I understand your concerns, but I'm afraid Grace is the only one who can decide to cancel her contract."

"Oh well, if that's all it takes. Then come on, girls, our work here is done," Becca said, trying to pull the others from his office.

Sam rose from his seat. "If you don't mind me asking, can you tell me why you don't want your sister to find love?"

The others were already out the door. Only Quinn turned to hold his gaze. "Our sister will find love, without your contract and without you setting her up on dates. We can guarantee that."

"How?"

"We're psychic." Quinn pressed her lips together in a pinched smile before she walked out.

Sam turned back to the window to find Grace still watching him with those ridiculous binoculars. A wall full of men stood behind her, also with binoculars. Two were big and beefy, and what the hell were they wearing? Were those kilts? The two other men were just as big. They must be the husbands of the four who had just left, and possibly a friend, considering Sam hadn't heard that Becca was engaged, and Sam heard everything about his neighbors. Those guys sure did have their hands full. Laughter erupted from his lips.

Chapter 3

Sam pulled up outside the little beach house and grabbed the envelope from his passenger seat. He'd never be the type of man to strong-arm any woman into keeping a contract with him. No matter how beautiful she was. He jogged up to the door, rang the bell, and tapped the envelope against his palm. The sweet smell of roses from her garden drifted to his nose, making him look down. He spotted the zombie garden gnomes and grinned.

The front door swung open, and Grace stood there with wide eyes and with a toothbrush hanging out of her mouth. A tiny bit of toothpaste dripped from the crease of her lips onto her shirt.

"Cm in," she mumbled and left the door open for him to follow.

He took his cue and stepped inside the cozy home, shutting the door behind him. The smell of fresh-baked cookies drifted to his nose as Grace disappeared down a hall. A laptop sat open on the couch. A book lay open across the armrest, holding her spot, and a blanket lay nearby. He spotted the plate of cookies next to her seat. If this was Grace's life, no wonder she'd come to him. All she needed was a glass of wine and a cat.

Grace re-emerged minutes later. "I'm sorry, my sisters came back and told me that I was the one that had to cancel the contract and I forgot to call."

"Not a problem." He held out the envelope as his gaze took her in. Her black yoga pants had a small pair of red lips on the hip. Her matching tank top had a wet spot where the toothpaste had landed. She was a cute mess. "I voided your contract."

"Thanks." The smile she gave him didn't reach her eyes as she took the envelope and tossed it on the table. "You could have just sent it to the office or called and I would have picked it up. I'm sorry about my sisters storming your office."

"It's not a problem." He nodded toward the couch. "Big plans?"

"Nope. A little book boyfriend and a glass of wine."

His lips twitched, trying as he might not to smile that he'd gotten the wine part right, but not the cat.

"You?"

"I'm still heading out of town for a family wedding, which is why I decided to bring the contract. If you don't have any big plans, maybe you'd still like to join me. I hate to attend those. No pressure, since we cancelled the contract."

"You don't strike me as the kind of guy in need of a date," she said, tossing the same words at him that he'd used on her.

"Touché. I'm not. I thought if you'd still like to go, maybe I could give you some pointers on what to look for in a guy, like how to spot the married ones who conveniently forgot to wear their ring, or the ones that are just out looking for a good time. You know. The kind you should avoid, if you're wanting a serious relationship. There should be plenty there for us to work with. Free food, champagne, and advice. No strings attached."

"I've never heard of a wedding lasting a week. What else did you have planned?"

"I'm thankful it's only a week. I'm the best man."

Grace wet her lips. "Aren't you worried that I'll ruin your chances with a bridesmaid?"

He chuckled. "I'm hoping you do."

She studied him, and he didn't know what she saw in his eyes or on his face, but something like sympathy crossed hers. "Been there, done that, three times in fact. Let me pack a bag."

"Seriously?" His mouth parted.

"Yeah. Sounds like fun. No strings. I've got claws, and I'm not afraid to get dirty. I'll keep those hoes away from the Italian sausage, and it would serve my sisters right, the way they think they can manage my life."

"Sausage?"

"Never mind." She waved his question away. "Make yourself comfortable and give me ten minutes." She quickly moved back down the hall.

Sam sat on the couch and clasped his hands while he glanced around the room. Family pictures filled the top of her bookshelf. Books, just like the one lying open on her sofa, filled the rest of the shelves. He picked up the book she was reading and glanced at cover of a half-dressed woman with a man kissing her chest.

He turned to where she'd left off and read. His jeans tightened as his cock hardened behind his zipper with every heated word of the hero and heroine having sex. When did they start putting porn on pages? He'd been so engrossed with every word and every detail he hadn't heard her return.

"Good stuff, huh?"

"I'm sure some of their positions defy the laws of gravity."

"Yum. I hadn't read that part. I'll take it with me." She grinned like a woman ready to pull out sex toys and grabbed the book. She flipped it around and scanned the words. Any man would be crazy not to date this woman. Maybe it was the sex scene or the way she'd snatched the book from his hands and devoured the page in two seconds flat, but she was everything he imagined she'd be.

She snapped the book closed. "Those positions are doable for a woman that does yoga. You just need a flexible partner and a strong guy."

"Do you do yoga?"

"I grew up doing gymnastics. I've twisted my body in all kinds of directions. Yoga is a piece of cake."

As if his erection hadn't been hard enough, it now was pressed painfully against his zipper. Why was this woman still single?

Grace walked over to the bookshelf and grabbed another book. She pressed it against his chest. "You'll like this one."

She released the book, and he had no choice but to catch it. "What's the plot?"

"A guy, a girl, who cares. You'll learn some new positions in that sucker. Even I was surprised. You want to impress your partner? Take notes. These books are written by women, for women. That's my tip for you."

"Says the woman still looking for love."

"Maybe if a guy took the time to read these books, there might be a better pool, or at least a lot more satisfied women. Win/win. You should make that book a required read before signing your male clients. You can thank me later."

"I'll keep that in mind." Was there no filter? A lesser man would have blushed, but he found himself oddly intrigued.

"Seriously?" She looked surprised.

"No."

She shrugged. "Your loss. Are you ready?"

Was he?

Chapter 4

"Nice jet. Where are we going?" she asked as the jet took flight.

"Texas."

"Oh, that doesn't sound so bad. Hot and steamy like Florida, only...bigger."

"Everything's bigger in Texas," he said, opening his briefcase.

"A girl can only hope." She leaned back and watched the passing clouds. Sam appeared to be a normal guy. Maybe too fixated on his work, but she guessed he had to be to run a successful company. She nudged his elbow. Getting him to loosen up and ditch the boring paperwork was going to take a miracle. "Sam, have you ever joined the mile-high club?"

"No. Are you offering?"

"Not yet." She smiled. "Are you packing?"

"Excuse me?"

"Sausage casing."

He looked perplexed. Was she speaking a foreign language?

"Condoms."

He stuffed his paperwork back into his briefcase and shut it. "What is it with you referring to a penis as sausage?"

She shrugged. "Would you prefer wanker, knob head, snickerdoodle? I'm open to suggestions. I thought we should have a code name, you know...for when you're giving me tips."

Sam unbuckled his seatbelt, stood, and held out his hand.

"What are you doing?"

"It's obvious you're sexually frustrated and in dire need of an anatomy lesson."

As if he could embarrass her. Hadn't he yet figured out that it took a lot to embarrass her? She unhooked her belt and rose without taking his hand. She closed the distance between them. "May I touch you?"

"Be my guest." His lips twitched as he held out his arms.

Grace grabbed his crotch. "This is a cock, shaft, dick. Whatever the guy likes to hear that turns him on. She gently squeezed the hardening shaft. "One of those works for you. I can tell." She winked and moved her hand to his chest. "Pecs. Good for scratching and kissing. Unless the woman is like me. I like to bite and leave a mark." She touched the tip of her tongue to her upper lip and moved her hands down his arms. "Muscles. Great for holding when pressed against the wall. Girls like that." She stepped closer and grabbed his ass. "And this is an ass, nice and tight. Women like to dig their heels into a man's ass to get them moving. Do I need to prove I know my own body? Because I can."

"Sausage. We'll stick with sausage." He pulled her closer and leaned to whisper in her ear. "Next time you touch a man like that, be prepared to follow through."

"Who said I wouldn't?"

"I think I've misjudged you, Grace."

"Am I hopeless? Are you ready to turn the jet around or make me jump without a parachute?"

"Just the opposite. I think you're the perfect date to this wedding."

She didn't know if it was a compliment or a dis, and she didn't care. She was on a pretty jet with a pretty man who was going to tell her exactly what she needed to do to snag a man. A little tit for tat so her bestie could compare tactics.

Sam kept his briefcase closed the rest of the flight, and she dropped the subject of sex. Hours later they'd landed and were in a rental SUV headed down some dusty, bumpy roads.

"Are the bride and groom one of your successful matches?"

"I guess you could say they met because of me." He swallowed hard, and his fingers turned white around the steering wheel. There was a story in there somewhere, and she'd poke until it flowed out like an untapped keg.

"Clue me in. What am I walking into?"

"Sarah is my ex, and she's marrying my brother."

"Nooo. And you agreed to be in the wedding?"

"He's my brother."

"Don't worry. I've got this." Grace nodded and turned to see horses running alongside the SUV. Their well-groomed coats glistened in the sunlight as their tails flew out behind them, hooves thundering against the packed earth.

The SUV pulled through the iron gates. The sign above it read Wymore Plantation. The hotel sat nestled on the greenest grass she'd seen since landing. The place was stunning. The steps led up to a landing with a concrete waterfall. Grecian columns surrounded the front of the plantation home with white wicker seats strategically placed. Off in the distance, there was a barn with cows, and horses out in a pasture. She squeezed his bicep. "You didn't tell me there'd be animals."

"You didn't ask?" he said more like a question than a statement.

"I've got this thing..." she said, making a circle motion with her hand, trying to stop her throat from closing at the site. "I don't like animals, but they seem to like me. I swear I must put out an animal pheromone of some sort. They gravitate to me wherever I go. It's like they're stalking me as their prey."

He took her hand and removed her nails from his arm. "They're corralled. They can't get to you."

She gave a slow nod and took several deep breaths. "Promise?"

"I promise." He gave her a reassuring smile. "Time to put on your game face. They're waiting for us on the veranda."

Grace slipped out of the SUV and waited for Sam to grab their bags. They started up the twenty steps. Why anyone would make you climb a mountain to get to a hotel, she'd never understand. With each step, Grace got a better look at the bride and groom.

"Honey, you didn't tell me you are a twin."

He glanced at her and smiled. "Are you going to be able to tell us apart? She couldn't."

Grace broke out in a fit of laughter and had to cling to his arm for the last five steps. She tried to suppress her giggles and ignore the couples' annoyed looks. That wasn't the last time she'd be seeing them.

"Is something funny?" The woman holding the hand of Sam's look alike asked. Her brow rose and a look of disdain crossed her face. She was clearly not amused.

He dated you. The words were on the tip of Grace's tongue, but she bit them back. "I was just remembering the pilot coming on over the loud speaker and asking Sammy to quit making the plane shake. I tried to tell him that the staff would know, but you know Sammy. He's insatiable and has the stamina of a two-year-old in a candy store."

"I can't keep my hands off her," Sam announced. "Grace, I'd like to introduce you to my brother, Richard, and his fiancée, Sarah Singletary."

"Nice to meet you both." Grace shook their hands and held Sarah's a second longer and winked. "Thank you."

"For what?" Sarah said, slipping her hand free.

"For Sammy, of course." She smiled over at Richard. "No offense."

"None taken. I've always wanted Sam to be happy."

She bet he did. Was that before or after he played hide the salami? Oh, that was another one she should ask Sam if he preferred.

"If you'll excuse us, we'd like to get checked in. It's been a long day." Sam gestured toward the doors and waited until they were alone in the lobby before he spoke. "Was that necessary?"

"No, but it was fun." Grace cleared her throat, and she stretched her jaw from the fake smile. "Would you like me to tone it down?"

Sam walked to the counter and pulled out his wallet. He gave his name and slid his credit card to the man behind the desk.

"Absolutely not," he said, pulling Grace into his arms. He buried his head into her shoulder. "Richard and Sarah are still watching us."

Grace rested her palms on his cheeks and stared deeply into his eyes with their mouths only inches apart. She licked her lips. "I think they're still in shock, or maybe Sarah's regretting that I got the brother with all the stamina. That's another thing girls like."

She pressed her mouth to his in a slow, sensual kiss that would make her momma blush and her Aunt Betty hoot and holler for more. Mint exploded in her mouth as his cologne cocooned her in his exquisite smell. His tongue danced with hers as the heat between them grew. If he was faking his need and desire, then he was better than she thought. A kiss like that was for the record books. He took what she so willingly gave and pulled her closer, holding her back as he bent her slightly over his arm.

"Hmm hmm." The desk clerk cleared his throat. "Excuse me."

Sam broke the kiss but stared deep into Grace's eyes, as if just the sight mesmerized him. "Yeah."

"Sir, your room."

"Right." He turned back to the desk and glanced at her once more before shaking his head. "Our room."

"Our room." Grace wiggled her brows and slowly licked her lips, savoring his taste. It wasn't until he had the room key and the luggage that she noticed the couple was gone. One point for Grace and Sam, officially team Grasam. Maybe she should get them some shirts made. That might piss the bride off just a bit more. The thought had merit.

Chapter 5

Grace stood in front of the window looking down at the glistening pool twinkling beneath the night stars. A few guests were sitting in the chairs drinking beers. A couple was in the pool making out.

Sam stood next to her and glanced down. "I didn't peg you for a voyeur."

"Look, she has her own flotation devices." Grace grinned. The woman's fake breasts were about the size of two oversized melons. "Maybe that's what I'm lacking." Grace cupped her breasts and squeezed.

"You have plenty," Sam said, crossing the room and unzipping his suitcase.

She moved to hers and pulled out her black gel-filled Tomb Raider-style pushup bra. "I know how to fake it."

"Lesson number one. Men like real women, not the plastic kind. A handful is all that's needed, and judging by your top, I'd say you have more than enough to satisfy any man."

"You must be a leg man."

"I don't discriminate. All parts of a woman are beautiful. Would you like me to demonstrate?"

"You want to fill me up, don't you, big guy?"

He took her hand and moved her to look at herself in front of a mirror. "Your eyes are the windows to your soul. Any man worth a damn will compliment how beautiful they are." He cleared his throat and rested his palms on her shoulders. "Your skin is silky smooth. Men should be begging to kiss every inch of it."

Her heart skipped a beat as he gestured to her breasts in the reflection, being a gentleman, he rested his palms on her ribcage just beneath her breasts without touching. Damn it if she didn't want to move grab them and put them where she'd hoped he would touch.

"Those are plenty big enough. More than a handful and just right."

She wiggled her ass against him and felt his arousal. He'd be in need of a cold shower soon. For that matter, so would she.

He moved his hands down over her hips, sending shivers down her spine. Her mouth went dry as she thought about those hands roaming her body sans clothing. "Your curves are womanly and perfect, in all the right places."

"You're good for my ego. Will you come over and remind me every morning? I could make it worth your while." She chuckled as he gave her a little squeeze.

"You know what I like best about you, Grace Thatcher?" he asked, meeting her gaze in the mirror. "Your mind. The way you find humor in everything, and the way you'll help people you barely know. There is absolutely no reason you should still be single, and I have every intention of helping you rectify that."

"I'd look like your ex if I started man-hunting when I already suggested I was here with you."

"You're nothing like my ex," he said before releasing her. He grabbed his clothes and walked into the bathroom.

Holy mother of guacamole. He'd left her body tingly, and she stared after him long after he had shut the door. This man was bad. So very bad. This vacation was going to be fun. Women probably ate that shit up, and she'd been one of them. He was a living, breathing Casanova. He'd been going to give her pointers in how to spot the players in a bunch of available men. Maybe she should have been asking for tips on the art of seduction. She was already taking mental notes. Only women would find a way to flunk, just so they could take the class again. She would.

Grace grabbed her clothes and slipped into a pair of boy shorts and a tank top before grabbing her toothbrush. She wrapped her knuckles on the door and waited for him to answer.

"Come in." He hollered out.

"Hope you don't mind, but I'd really like to brush my teeth."

"You don't strike me as a prude, Grace, and I'm sure you've seen your share of naked men."

"You'd be right." She chuckled. "You know, your talents are going to waste sitting behind a desk."

"What talents are those?" he asked from the steam fogging the glass shower door. Pity.

"Seduction 101."

He chuckled as she wet her toothbrush and slathered on the toothpaste.

"That wasn't a seduction, Grace. That was me complimenting your assets."

"Assets, right." She had plenty of those. Just ask her sister. The seams in her favorite jeans would never be the same because of the size of Grace's assets. She brushed her teeth and rinsed her mouth as the shower water cut off. She hopped up on the sink counter. "Why are you still single? Are you afraid of getting burned again?"

"I'm busy helping others."

The door opened, and Sam stood there, in all his manliness, as he grabbed a towel and wiped his face. The biggest, thickest sausage she'd ever seen was standing fully erect.

"You should register that thing as a choking hazard."

Sam secured the towel around his waist. "I've never had any complaints."

"You must date porn stars." That would explain a lot. Maybe he'd starred in one she hadn't seen. She'd be checking her collection when she got home.

"Foreplay is a must." He winked as he moved to the counter and grabbed his own toothbrush.

"You're a very secure guy. If I were you, I'd join a nudist camp and be walking around naked like Tarzan. Screw the leaf covering your junk. You'd probably make the average nudist feel a bit insecure. You could be king."

The creases around his eyes deepened as he smiled around his toothbrush. The heat in the bathroom was smoldering as she jumped down from the counter. Another minute and she'd be asking him if she could make a mold or take pictures. No way would her sisters take her at her word.

"You must be a native Texan." Everything was bigger in Texas. He was proof.

She left him in the bathroom and slid into bed. He was practically a stranger, yet oddly, she didn't feel any awkwardness. Maybe it was the lack of expectations on both their parts, or the fact he'd already felt her up and she'd seen his meat. Either way, her heart sped up at the thought of what else the week would bring.

****

Grace had dreamt of Sam's wanker the entire night. It had been like a monster, the size of buildings, as it trampled through the city pounding everything in its path. She'd slipped out of the bed and changed into a pair of yoga pants, a tank top, and her running shoes. There was only one way to ease her sexual frustration that didn't include taming the one-eyed monster. She had to run, long and hard, to the point of exhaustion, and that was exactly what she planned to do.

She pulled her hair up into a ponytail and grabbed a room key before slipping out the door. The hotel was quiet as she made her way down the steps, slipping the room key inside her sports bra. The sun was just starting to peek over the horizon. The animals, secure behind a gate, stared at her and inched closer as she took off down the dirt road. With each pounding step, Grace's heart raced while the animals kept the pace running with her. There was something about her that attracted the wild beasts, as if she were their catnip or sent out some crazy, horny animal pheromone. If she could bottle it up and sell it to those people who bred stallions or bulls, she be a billionaire.

Men on horseback in the distance watched as sheep took off toward the fence. They looked stunned as they sat atop their horses. A few of the horses bucked as if wanting to join in on the chase.

Two miles away, with an audience of animals, she turned around and headed back toward the hotel. Her lungs burned with her strides. Neither the run nor the animals did anything to help her forget the view of male perfection Sam had gifted to her. Damn him for teasing her.

****

Sam woke up as the sunrise glinted in through the curtains. He rolled into his pillow to cover his eyes and hugged the one next to him. He inhaled her strawberry scent. Grace.

He absentmindedly reached across the bed. His palm landed on the empty cool sheets. He opened his eyes and sat up. Grace wasn't in the room. "Where the hell did she go?"

Sam got dressed, grabbed the room key and headed downstairs in search of strong coffee and his missing date. The coffee came first, and he stepped outside, where two cowboy-hat-wearing groomsmen were standing on the veranda along with a few of Sarah's bridesmaids.

"I've never seen anything like it," Mike, one of the groomsman, muttered and tipped his hat back farther on his head as if removing it from his blocking his view

"Who's she here with?" Stan, another groomsman, asked.

"Who cares? Do you see her tight little body? I could bury myself in that for days and never come up for air," another replied.

"She's no one special," Mary, one of the bridesmaids, said while taking a seat in one of the chairs with the other bridesmaids. She'd been the one in the pool the night before with Stan.

The guys were too mesmerized to even respond. Sam glanced in the direction they were staring and found Grace running. Inside the fence, every farm animal in close proximity was keeping up with her and jostling to be closer to the fence. He set his coffee down and planted his hands on his hips as she neared. When she'd said animals liked her, that had been the understatement of the century. She jogged up the steps. Her gaze slid across each face before landing on his. Her lips twisted into a smile as she jumped into his arms, wrapping her legs around his waist. He had to brace himself against falling backward.

"Good, you're up." She smiled down at him and planted a hard kiss on his lips. Her hands slid into his hair as she tilted her head, deepening the kiss. If he hadn't realized it was just for show, he might have pinned her to the wall and taken her right there. She smelled of sweet sweat and strawberries. Her hair was slicked back, and her clothes clung to her body. The move did more than draw the attention of the onlookers. It woke his body up in a way the coffee hadn't.

Too soon she broke the kiss. "I've had my workout. Are you ready for yours?" She winked. Damn, she was good.

"Absolutely," he said, turning to carry her back into the hotel. He stopped just beneath the doorframe. "Mike, could you tell my brother I'll catch him after breakfast?"

"Sure."

"Better make it lunch," she called out and giggled as the doors shut behind them.

She slid down his body and walked with him back to the elevators, not saying a word until they were nestled inside.

"Sorry about the stink. I smell like I've been wrestling with the hogs. I could tell those women were the bridesmaids just by their looks. They looked ready to jump me."

"They weren't the only ones. The guys are groomsmen, and I can tell you that you've made several fans."

"Good to know." She smiled and rubbed at her aching calves. "Did you know this place is haunted? And by haunted, I mean crowded with spirits. In the fields, on the porch, and there was even one in our room."

"Why didn't you say something before now?"

She shrugged as the elevator dinged and the doors slid open to their floor. "I normally ignore it, but running is like my meditation. All kinds of things smack me in the face, and I'm not talking about the jet-sized bugs."

That was out of the blue. For a while, he'd forgotten her profession.

He opened the door to their room and let her pass. Before she made it to the bathroom, she was wrestling with her sports bra, trying to peel the thing from her body. Her arms got twisted in the fabric as it caught on her head.

He grinned as he took in her struggle while flashing him her breasts. "You need help?"

"Nah, I'm taking a page from your book, learning how to be more confident and comfortable in my own skin."

"There's nothing shy about you, is there?"

"You think I'm bad, my sister, Quinn, is worse."

From the looks of her struggle, she was failing miserably. She was dancing like a blind chicken while trying to kick off her shoes at the same time her face was still covered. Her breasts bounced as she jumped before she tripped on her shoe. He was quick to catch her before she cracked her head on the dresser. His arms encased her as he pulled her flush against his body.

"Stop moving."

She stood motionless, only tugging twice more, unsuccessfully, at the top.

He slipped the fabric free from beneath her chin and tugged it off. "You need lessons on the art of stripping."

"I'll look for a class when we get home. Maybe pole dancing, too. That sounds like fun."

Her cheeks were a pretty shade of pink, and her chest heaved. It took every ounce of willpower not to take her breast into his mouth. Sam squatted in front of her and peeled off her other shoe and both socks.

He slowly rose and stood in front of her. His fingers toyed with the waistband of her yoga pants. "Do you need help with these?"

She slipped his fingers free. "I'm not sure I'm ready for that lesson." She nibbled her lip between her teeth. "You'd end up missing the entire week of wedding festivities."

"It would be worth it," he whispered in her ear.

Chapter 6

Grace took an extra cold shower to douse the horny flames raging her body. She'd been two seconds away from swinging on Tarzan's vine. Her inner Aunt Betty flag was flapping in the wind. She wasn't here to hook up with Sam. She'd been meaning to gain insider tips on how he ran his business. Hell, he'd been her target from day one, and now she was damned if she didn't want him to hit the bullseye. She needed to get them both out of the room, and preferably, wearing clothes. She took her time getting ready, applying a little makeup and slipping into a sundress after she had dried her hair.

The heat from the morning sun had been almost unbearable, and she wouldn't risk looking like a drunk raccoon if the festivities were outside. Wearing more than a slip of material would be like torture. She walked out of the room to find Sam on the bed, leaning against the headboard, reading the book she'd given him at her house.

His hand rested on his stomach.

"Good book, right?"

"I...." He glanced at her and then back to the pages. "You might be on to something about making this required reading."

Grace grinned, and estimated by the number of pages what scene he might be on. She'd read it plenty of times to have the whole thing memorized. Within the first few pages, the heroine had met the hero in the bar and he'd given her an orgasm without breaching the barrier of her clothes. Sam hadn't even gotten to the good stuff.

"Any man who can produce pleasure without getting naked needs to be cloned."

Sam chuckled and set the book on the nightstand. "I bet you're starving."

He had no idea. Her gaze went to the bulge in his jeans, and her mouth watered. "I could eat."

"Let's go." He stood, then grabbed his wallet and the room key. "We'll probably get scolded since we missed the group breakfast."

"Take it like a champ that scored the winning touchdown." She smiled as they headed for the elevators. "They all believe you did."

The elevator doors slid open. Sarah and Richard stood inside. She had her arms crossed over her chest and was giving him her back as he pleaded behind her. His words were cut off when he realized the elevator had stopped and they were standing there.

"We were just coming to find you." Richard said.

"Sorry." Grace smiled like a woman who'd been up to no good. She had. "I made him lose track of time."

Sarah's gaze narrowed as she dropped her stance, placed her hand around Richard's waist, and leaned into his side. "We know how that is, don't we, babe?"

Sure she did. What had Sam seen in Sarah? They stepped into the elevator and hit the button for the lobby.

"What's on the agenda today?" Sam asked and rested his arm around Grace's shoulders. She pasted a smile on her face and hugged his waist.

"We have tux fittings in an hour, and Sarah is going with the girls to pick up their dresses," Richard answered.

It was hard to imagine Sarah mixing up the two men. Grace could tell them apart, and she'd known one for an entire day and the other in passing. Richard oozed a calm persona, one that it would take a lot of prodding to piss off, whereas Sam was nothing if not passionate. They were as different as granny panties and a thong.

"Grace, you should go with them," Richard prodded.

Sarah's mouth parted before she narrowed her eyes up at Richard. Grace should go if for no other reason than to aggravate the one woman who'd cheated on Sam. Maybe rub her nose in the fact that she'd lost out. Still, the idea excited her about as much as watching old men play chess. No, thank you. Grace had already been crowned queen and taken Sarah's king. Checkmate, or was it considered game, set, match? It didn't matter. Grace was winning.

"That's okay. I'll just hang out by the pool and work on my tan. After last night, and the morning we had, I'm as spent as a cowgirl riding bareback for a month."

"You did whistle Dixie." Sam leaned down and kissed her lips.

"Bring me back a black cowboy hat for my ride tonight."

"You don't want white?"

Grace ran her palms over Sam's biceps. "Honey, we both know I'm not an angel."

The elevator opened, and Sam escorted Grace out and toward the restaurant.

"She's a tacky two-bit whore," Sarah whispered loud enough for Grace to hear.

"Look who's talking."

Anger welled up in Grace's stomach. Cuss words lingered on her tongue. Her Quinn-like inner demon was ready to take flight. The bitch had some nerve. Grace spun around, ready to pounce. Sam's arm tightened around her waist, and he turned her back toward the restaurant, laying his arm tightly over her shoulder.

"Ignore her," Sam whispered into her ear.

"I'll meet you outside in an hour," Richard called after them.

Sam raised his hand in an acknowledgment without looking back.

Grace spotted several ghosts in the dining area. A smile split her lips as her mind raced with all kinds of new ways that she could help the bride remember the special event.

Sam pulled out a chair for her to sit and leaned down to whisper in her ear. "What's that look for?"

"I'm imaging the wedding pictures when I drown her in a vat of orange Jell-O after sending all of the hotel ghosts to terrorize her."

"There's never a dull moment with you."

"What are you going to tell you parents about us? I assume they'll eventually be showing up."

"They'll be showing up in a couple of days. I guess we really should get our story straight. I'm sure the guys are going to grill me too."

"You could always tell them I'm a streetwalker you picked up at the airport. Sarah already thinks I'm one."

"She's one to talk, jumping from one brother's bed to the other. Shit like that should be illegal. Besides, no one would buy that version. I own a successful dating agency."

The waiter appeared, took their order and quickly left. The morning breakfast crowd had thinned out so their conversation was somewhat private.

"How about telling them I was a client?"

He shook his head. "That would make you seem desperate. They'd never buy it, at least the guys wouldn't."

"You could always tell them that we met when you called Linked Inc."

Sam's eyes widened, almost as if in horror. That was an interesting look that needed exploring.

"That one would never fly either. They'd never believe I'd call a psychic."

"Why wouldn't they believe you called a psychic?" She asked as if she hadn't heard all of the reasons why people didn't believe in her and her job.

"They just wouldn't." He said and quickly changed the subject. "How about a friend of a friend?"

She'd let it slide for now. The waiter appeared with their drink orders, and she took a sip of her sweet tea. "Do we have any friends in common?"

Sam sipped his hot coffee as an elderly female ghost floated to the table wearing a flowered dress. Tell them you met through Aunt Annie.

"Aunt Annie said we can use her as how we met."

Sam spit his coffee, quickly grabbed a napkin, and wiped at his mouth.

"You look surprised." Grace grinned and removed her elbows from the table as food was placed in front of both of them.

"Did you just say Aunt Annie?"

Grace glanced up at the woman. "Yeah. Flowered dress, round face, nice smile. She looks….sweet."

"Don't let her looks fool you. That woman could have been one of your relatives."

"Aw," Grace said and smiled at the lady. "I like her already."

"Well, you should. You both have something in common."

Grace let her eyes slide over the woman's features and apparel to see if she could spot what he was talking about. Nope, nothing in appearance. "You'll have to fill me in because I don't see it."

"Neither of you like Sarah."

Grace chuckled as Annie held up a locket that was resting around her neck.

"You really are a psychic?" He asked.

"I really am." Grace tried to use her pleasing tone that her momma taught her, but her answer probably came out more Quinn style. He's allowed to be a skeptic. She reminded herself. Most people are.

"I didn't mean..."

"It's okay." Grace gave him a reassuring smile. "She's showing me her locket. Is that significant?"

Sam cut into his omelet and lifted the bite to his lips. "I bought her a new one to replace the one that was stolen."

"One was stolen?" Grace asked him and looked up at Annie. "I'm sorry."

"It was my fault," Sam said, taking another bite. He didn't elaborate until he swallowed. "She insisted on giving me a graduation party, and one of the people attending, stole it."

"Did you ever figure out who took it?" Grace asked.

"Nope, but the entire wedding party was there that night," he said, clearing his throat.

They ate a hurried breakfast, in easy banter, after that conversation. A few of Sam's other dead relatives floated around the dining room, but after the look he'd given her upon hearing about Annie, he might have busted a blood vessel knowing other relatives had shown up. Maybe ghosts at weddings weren't as normal for everyone else as they were for Grace's family.

Sam held her hand as he walked her back into the lobby where his brother and the rest of his groomsmen were waiting. He slowed and pulled her into his arms, smiling down at her face. "What are you going to do today?"

"Maybe hang out by the pool, take a nap, or talk a cowboy out of his hat."

Sam's lips twisted into a smile. His eyes sparkled as he stared at her. "I'm sure that wouldn't be too hard, but don't bother. We can pick one up in town tonight after dinner. I thought it would be nice to show you the town since you've never been here."

"I'll hold you to that," she grinned.

Chapter 7

Grace left them in the lobby and hopped on the elevator to head back to the room. She had some hours to kill, and that would give her plenty of time to finish the book she'd started.

As the doors to the elevator opened to her floor, she was greeted by a loud, ear-piercing scream. She stepped out directly into the path of a woman shrieking, a towel haphazardly pulled around her body. Grace barely caught the woman and herself from falling on their asses.

"Are you okay?" Grace asked.

The woman's face was covered in a green goop beauty mask that had hardened to look like concrete on her face. It was complete with cracks that reminded her of the roads back home. Her chest was heaving as she looked back toward the open door of her room. A look of horror was etched across her face.

"I had just stepped into the shower when I heard a noise. I opened the shower curtain and a ghost was standing there watching me." The woman clutched the towel tighter to her trembling body. Goosebumps covered her bare arms.

A peeping ghost. Perfect. There went her idea for a pleasant afternoon of catching up with a certain hero. The ravishing would have to wait.

"I'm Grace Thatcher, room 404 and I'm a medium. It just so happens to be your lucky day. I know how to get rid of ghosts. Do you want me to kick his ass out?"

She nodded as if words eluded her.

Grace walked in through the opened door to find the layout of the woman's room was identical to her own. The curtains were pulled closed. The light was on, as was the television. The lady in the towel stood at the door as if afraid to cross the threshold.

"He was in the bathroom." The woman's voice came out as a squeak.

Grace headed for the bathroom to find the ghost still in there, as if he'd been waiting for the woman to return. "Listen Perv, that lady doesn't want you here, so you're gonna have to go."

The ghost turned toward her with a sheepish grin on his face. No.

She heard the word loud and clear in her mind, as if the ghost had said it out loud. "Fine. You want me to do this the hard way?"

The ghost's laughter rang loud in her head.

"You can't say I didn't warn you." Grace spun on her heels and left the room. The woman in the towel followed her across the hall and into Grace's room.

"Did he leave?"

"Not yet, but he will." Grace grabbed a hotel robe from her bathroom and handed it to the woman before she grabbed a lighter, sage, a small cigarette-type ashtray to catch the ashes, and salt from her purse. She never left home without it.

"What are you going to do with that?" The woman asked while securing the robe at her waist.

"Give you back your space," she answered, as if the answer was obvious.

Returning to the room, she found the ghost hovering above the bed. She lit the sage and was rewarded with a glare from the ghost. He knew what was coming next. "You know what this does?"

He didn't budge. He didn't disappear or move as if in a standoff. Grace moved to the corner of the room and smudged the corner. She made quick work, moving through the room while she demanded her intentions in her mind. I reclaim this space. All others energies MUST leave in the name of the Father, The Son, and the Holy Spirt.

She continued with saging the room until she'd moved the ghost out the open door. He stood just beyond the threshold as Grace grinned and slammed it in his face, saging that as well. She quickly layered salt at the door and along the window. "You should be good now."

"Is he gone?"

"For now, until the cleaning lady vacuums up your salt." Grace dabbed the burning embers of the sage stick into the tray just as the smoke alarm started to blare in the rooms.

Grace glanced around the room and spotted the smoke detector. She hurried to the phone and dialed the front desk.

No one answered.

"You might want to get dressed while I go explain what happened."

The woman nodded and grabbed her clothes just as Grace left the room. Grace didn't wait. She jogged down the emergency stairs pushing past the other hotel guests and out into the lobby. She spotted the man that had checked her and Sam in. He was holding the front door open as people rushed out.

"There's no fire. It's a false alarm."

"What? Were you smoking in your room?"

"I don't smoke," Grace argued. "A ghost was harassing one of your guests, and I got rid of him by saging."

"By what?"

She shook her head. "It's like incense."

The fully clothed, frightened woman approached them, and the desk clerk stood taller. "Mrs. Wymore. It's a false alarm."

Wymore? Grace tilted her head. "You own the place."

"I do. I'm Eleonore Wymore." She patted the desk clerk's arm. "Johnny, be a dear and call the fire department to let them know it's a false alarm and that we already know what happened."

"Yes, Ms., right away."

"If you own the place, why aren't you staying in the penthouse suite?"

Eleonore smiled and wrapped her arm around Grace's. "I got a call from my manager that we were having some paranormal issues, so I came to check it out myself. I took the room that was having the most activity. It frightened the guests before me so badly that they left in the middle of the night."

The alarm shut off and Johnny nodded with the phone still pressed to his ear as Eleonore led us both into the bar attached to the restaurant. "Why don't you tell me a bit more about what it is you do, Ms. Thatcher, while I have a drink to calm my nerves?"

"You can call me Grace."

Grace spend the next two hours talking to Eleonore and hearing about how the place had always been haunted, but even more so since renovations had started on the top floor and Eleonore had taken some heirlooms home from the attic. Grace told her a bit about all of the ghosts she'd seen since arriving. The conversation had morphed into the history of the place, and Grace lost track of time, sharing stories with Eleonore about the things they'd both experienced.

"I hope you two aren't getting sloshed," Sam said laying his palms on Grace's arm.

"Ah." Eleonore smiled. "You're here with Sam Stone. I should have guessed."

"You two know each other?" Grace asked.

"We grew up together," Sam said with a nod. "It's nice to see you, Ellie."

Eleonore rose from her seat. "You too, Sam. You're looking well." She gave a polite smile, and I had the feeling these two had some sort of deeper history, but who was I to pry. "If you and Grace need anything while you're here, don't hesitate to ask. I'm in Grace's debt. She helped me out of a jam."

"So I hear." Sam raised a brow as he looked at Grace. "I heard there was an issue with the fire detectors."

"Not an issue. I was banishing a ghost from her room," Grace said when standing.

"A ghost? Really?"

"I know what I saw, Sam," Eleonore exclaimed. "It was a ghost; Grace was a dear and sent it packing."

"She's right." Grace smiled and glanced at Eleonore. "It was a pleasure meeting you. I'm in town for the rest of the week for a wedding. Let me know if he comes around again. Only this time, we'll disable the fire alarms first."

"Yes. Next time, we should do that first."

"Let's hope there isn't a next time." Grace clasped her hands together. She really did hope that there wouldn't be, but even she knew how pesky spirits could be.

Chapter 8

"I hope you don't mind about the whole ghost debacle," Grace said while running a brush through her hair as she stared in the mirror above the dresser.

"Did anyone else know it was you?" He should have said something to ease her concerns. He knew what she was and what she did, but announcing it to everyone at the hotel hadn't been his plan. She was beautiful and stunning. He'd planned on questions about them as a couple, just not for her to give a performance of her career choice.

She laid the brush on the dresser and turned to look at him. The smile she'd worn since he returned had slipped. The shine in her eyes dimmed. "Would it bother you if they had?"

"No," he said and shook his head. He was being ridiculous. He knew it, and so did she. He'd brought her here, knowing full well, the possible ramifications.

"No," he repeated with more conviction. "It's what you do."

"It's a part of me, Sam. If that's a problem..."

"It's not." He closed the distance between them and cupped her cheek. His gaze softened, caressing her face before he let it travel down to her plump lips. The need to kiss her was overwhelming and yet, instead, he met her gaze again, wanting her to not only see and hear the sincerity in his words, but to know that he meant them.

"I know you're a medium. That wasn't what I meant when I said it's what you do. I meant that you help people. That's what you do. Just like you being here with me. That's who you are, and that's what I like about you."

"Good." She smiled brightly. "Because I like you too, but I won't change. This is me, for better or worse. I'll always be the oddball in the room, dealing with spirits and pissing off someone's ex."

"I wouldn't change a thing." He leaned down and pressed his lips to hers in a soft kiss, ruining the lip gloss she'd recently swiped on her lips. The floral scent of her shampoo teased his nose. Her beauty was unmatched, and her lip gloss tasted of his favorite fruit, delicate strawberries picked in the afternoon sun. It was true. He wouldn't change a thing about her. The grumble in her stomach was the only thing that had him breaking the kiss. The reminder that she needed substance, they both did if they were going to get through the rest of the week.

"You didn't tell me where we're going. Do I look okay?" She turned and fixed her lipstick in the mirror. Her jeans cupped her in all the right places. Her top was flirty and very Grace-like. She was the epitome of the girl next door, if the girl next door was sassy and delectable.

"You look perfect. Let's get you fed," he said leading her to the door with his hand on the small of her back.

****

The small restaurant wasn't what Grace expected. It was quaint and full of life. Bull horns hung from the wall along with autographed pictures of old western movie stars. A jukebox was in the corner; the music was soft and light. There was nothing five stars about the place, and yet, the ambiance made her feel welcome. Their table was near the windows, giving her the perfect view of downtown. Couples strolled by walking hand in hand. A family with kids, skipping and playing in front of them, walked by as they window shopped. The cars on the street were mainly dusty pickup trucks, and most of the men wore cowboy hats with tans that her sisters would pay big money to achieve. Everything about this place was real.

"This makes sense," she said glancing down at her open menu.

"What does?"

"You, here, your job. You want everyone to have what these people have. I can relate, and I admire that."

Sam glanced around, as if he were trying to see the magic that Grace could feel. But it wasn't something you could see, it was a feeling that was as unique as Sam.

"I've missed the place, not all the people in it, but the town. It has a certain charm."

"We should visit again; you know, when you aren't marrying your brother off to that tramp."

Sam smiled. This was the first time she'd seen him relax since they had landed. "We should."

They ordered, and Grace ate the best barbecue of her life. She dug into the slathered ribs as if her momma hadn't taught her any manners. The messy sauce held just the right amount of spice and twang, and the meat had been smoked to perfection. If she could bottle up the restaurant and take it home with her, she'd be a queen in Florida. She'd used five wet wipes on her hands and mouth before they left to stroll down Main Street.

A hat store sat on one of the corners, and she headed straight for it, yanking open the door. She grabbed the first black cowboy hat she came across and stuck it on her head before turning a smile at Sam. "Do you like this one?"

"Very cute," he said, leaning in to kiss her, only pausing to tilt the hat back on her head. He pressed his lips to hers. "Every cowgirl should have one."

"These aren't very convenient for kissing," she mumbled. "I'll need to practice so I don't knock you out with the brim."

"I'll be your guinea pig," he said pulling her body flush with his. The heat from his touch awakened her in all the right places as he lowered his lips to hers, only stopping when the bell above the door dinged again, announcing the arrival of more customers.

"You're hired." She teased and moved from his hold, trying on other hats until she found just the right one.

Sam picked up a hat and shoved it on his head. "I'll have you know, I take my job very seriously."

Grace smiled. "I would hope so." She smacked his ass as she headed for a rack of chaps. "I think I might need some of these too."

"I could see you in a pair of those." Sam wiggled his brows.

She shifted the clothes around looking for a pair in her size. "So what other best man duties are you required to attend?"

"The bachelor party, the rehearsal dinner, pictures, and the wedding."

Grace pulled out a pair of black chaps that matched the hat and glanced over her shoulder with a conspiratorial smile. "I think I'll need a lasso and whip to round out the look."

"I should be so lucky."

Lucky, he'd be getting, if she had her way. A few heated kisses wouldn't be enough to please her appetite, not after the way he'd wet it. They were in the gray zone, between friends and lovers. Hell, she'd settle for a one night stand. The pull had shifted after the first kiss. No way would she be leaving the great state of Texas without taking this cowboy for a test ride. Grace laid her purchases on the counter and bumped Sam's hip as he stood next to her. "I think a little luck could be arranged, before our trip is over."

Chapter 9

Sam didn't wait for the hotel door to close before he slipped the bags free from Grace's hands and let them drop to the floor. He pulled her into his arms and backed her against the wall. He took her lips in a heated kiss as his hands trailed a path from her hips to her ass. He squeezed, lifting her in his hold until he had her right where he wanted her. He ground the aching bulge behind his zipper that had been hardening since before he left the room. He hadn't planned on seducing her tonight, or at all for that matter. Grace wasn't a once and done type of girl, and damned if she didn't make him want more.

Grace squirmed in his hold as if trying to get closer. Their clothes were the only barrier stopping him from taking her, hot and heavy where they stood.

A knock on the door had them both stilling. He held her heated gaze as he spoke. "Yeah."

"I'm sorry to bother you two, but can I speak to Grace," Eleonore called out from the hallway.

Sam rested his forehead against Grace's. She mouthed the words. "I'm sorry."

"Yeah, just a second," he answered letting Grace's soft body slide down his. He waited for Grace to straighten her clothes before he pulled the door open.

"I'm so sorry," Eleonore exclaimed. Her cheeks were pink, her hair mussed. She looked flustered. "But I need your help. It seems the ghost didn't leave the hotel, just changed rooms and well....you'll just have to see for yourself."

"Of course." Grace smiled. "Let me just grab my things."

"This should only take a minute." Grace grabbed her purse and kissed Sam's lips before walking out into the hall.

"It might be a little longer than that," Eleonore exclaimed with a sigh.

Sam watched as the two hurried to the elevator and stepped inside. Grace turned and met his gaze. A look of regret filled her eyes. He knew that look. He felt the same way.

****

Grace was led down the corridor of the top floor and almost tripped on the carpet when she saw whose room they were going to. Richard and Sarah stood outside the door with their backs pressed against the hallway wall. Each of their faces were drained of color.

"Her," Sarah exclaimed. "You've got to be kidding me."

Grace grinned while pausing outside their door. She gestured over her shoulder with her thumb. "I can leave and let you deal with it, just say the word. As a matter of fact, I'm pretty sure Sam is in bed waiting for me."

"Please, fix this," Richard pleaded taking Sarah's hand. He ignored the angered look plastered on Sarah's face. "We can't stay in there unless you do. All the other rooms are taken."

Grace walked into the room to find it in shambles. Clothes were strewn across the bed and the floor. Perfume and makeup bottles on the dresser had toppled over.

"Did he make this mess?" She called out into the hall.

"We did that during an argument," Richard answered.

The love birds were fighting. That was news. Would there still be a wedding, or maybe it was truly Sam and Grace's lucky day, and they could be on the jet first thing in the morning.

Grace found the ghost from Eleonore's room hiding in the bathroom. What was it with this ghost and bathrooms?

"Okay, listen." She started to say, meeting the spirit's gaze. "We need to come to some form of agreement, or I'm going to have to banish you from the hotel for good, and I don't have the time or the patience. What's it going to take for you to leave the guests alone once and for all?"

He gestured toward the pocket watch lying on the counter.

"You can't even wear it; it belongs to Richard."

Not his. I'm looking for mine.

Now we were getting somewhere. The dude just wanted his watch, not that he could take it with him where he was going, but if it would get the guy to leave everyone alone. She'd help him.

"When did you die?"

1922

"Are you related to Eleonore?"

He nodded.

"Give me some time to find it, but wait for me in the attic. No more scaring people. Got it?"

The ghost vanished from site, and Grace spun around on her heels. The chance of her finding the pocket watch was slim to none, but she had to try. She walked out of the hotel room. "He's gone, but not for good. We have a momentary truce."

Sarah's eyes widened, Grace ignored her and turned to Eleonore. "He's your relative, and he's looking for a watch that belonged to him. I don't suppose you have any old relics laying around, do you?"

Eleonore smiled. "I have a ton of family heirlooms at my house. Come with me."

They started heading for the elevator when Richard called Grace's name, making her turn around.

"Thank you."

"You're welcome."

Four hours later, they'd found the watch tucked away in Eleonore's attic and returned to the hotel where Grace met with the ghost and returned his item after making him promise to quit scaring people. She'd warned him, if he didn't, she'd be returning with all of her sisters and they'd run his ghostly butt out of the building, for good.

When Grace returned to the room, Sam was sound asleep. His quiet snores filled the space as she changed clothes and slipped into bed next to him. As if he could feel her presence, he pulled her to his side and held her close.

"Did you save the day?" He mumbled.

"I did. Go back to sleep and I'll tell you all about it in the morning."

Sam grunted, and Grace fell asleep in his warm embrace.

Chapter 10

Grace woke up to find the bed beside her cold. A rose and a note lay on top of Sam's pillow. She swept the sleep from her eyes and held the note up to read.

You looked tired, and I didn't want to wake you. I ran into town with Richard to help find a gift for Sarah. Why don't you order room service and hang out by the pool. We should be back late this afternoon.

The bachelor party is tonight, so don't wear yourself out. I was hoping you'd be my date. Maybe we can sneak out early and try some of those gravity-defying positions that you love to read about.

That's just what Grace did. After breakfast, she slipped into her bathing suit, grabbed a towel and headed down to the pool. She lounged poolside, beneath one of the umbrella tables, sipping on a margarita for several hours, just enjoying the day. The sun and the sweltering heat could melt an ice cream cone in five seconds flat. Ice cream trucks probably didn't stick around these parts. Kids bounced in and out of the water as parents scolded about running and keeping their voices down. A few couples filled the chairs and the pool. It seemed this was the only water source around that promised to beat the Texas heat. Several shirtless cowboys wearing jeans and hats were in the distance, sitting astride horses while wrangling the animals she'd seen the other day.

Grace held the phone to her ear.

"Tell me again what possessed you to go to Texas," her best friend, Chloe, said.

"I'm helping Sam."

"You're on a first-name basis with my competition?" Chloe shrieked.

"I can't help that he's your competition." Grace frowned. "You know I'm a sucker for helping people in need, and he needed my help."

"Have you ever thought that maybe he knows what you had planned about getting some inside information on his business? You can't trust him."

"Relax, Chloe. He's not playing me. He needed a wingman, and I'm helping him. My sisters threatened him into canceling the contract. So...."

"So....no insider information."

"Afraid not, but I've come up with a few ideas how to get your dating agency back on track."

"Is this seat taken?" An older brunette woman asked while pointing to one of the empty chairs at Grace's table.

"I've got to go, Chloe. Tell my sisters I'll be back in a week." Grace hung up before Chloe could press for more than Grace was willing to share. She glanced up at the woman and gestured to a chair. "Help yourself."

"I didn't mean to interrupt your call."

"Oh, it's okay."

The woman sat down, slipped her big straw hat off her head, and set it on the table, just as a waiter appeared with an umbrella drink. The stranger smiled up at the server and slipped him some cash before he scurried off.

"I'll never get used to this Texas heat." The woman took a long draw from her drink while picking up her hat to fan her face.

"It's similar to Florida," Grace said.

"Oh, you're an out-of-towner. What brings you to these parts?" There was a hint of Texas twang in the woman's words.

"A wedding."

"I'm Annalise."

Annalise was beautiful. A southern lady that looked like she could dine with royalty in one breath, and in the next, could be just as comfortable out on the range with a bunch of cowboys.

The fine laugh lines around her eyes and mouth showed that she'd spent several years enjoying life. She was nowhere near as snobby as the bridesmaids that Grace had met.

"I'm Grace." Grace shook the woman's hand.

"Friend of the bride or the groom?" the woman asked.

"Neither," Grace said, sipping the last of her wine. "I'm here as moral support for the groom's brother."

"Does he not like weddings?" Annalise asked.

Grace shrugged. "I've known him for less than a week, but it was long enough to know that the bride royally screwed up when she screwed him over. He's a good guy. Decent, sexy, and he makes me laugh. What more could a woman want?"

"What more indeed," Annalise said. "If you don't mind me asking, what do you do for a living, Grace?"

"I'm a medium. I talk to dead people."

Annalise covered her mouth as she started choking on her drink.

"Is your drink too strong?"

"No, dear. Your answer just caught me off guard. I'm sure that you're the first medium I've ever met."

"Not what you were expecting, right? I get that a lot. We don't all wear cloaks and gobs of mascara." Grace grinned, leaned forward, and clasped her fingers together. "I've got some time to kill before Sam gets back. Would you like a reading?"

"Sam. Is that the groom's brother?"

"The whole reason I'm here." Grace smiled.

"I've never had a reading," Annalise answered.

Grace tried her best to block out the other people around the pool and concentrate on the woman. She could feel the uncertainty rolling off Annalise in waves. "It's a bit hard to concentrate with the crowd, but let's see what I can get."

Grace took a deep breath, inhaling the calm and exhaling the chaos. She'd taken several before one of the woman's relatives showed up.

"A man," Grace said. "Dark hair, liked his suits and ties. Very distinguished.

Says his name is Samuel." Grace met the woman's gaze. "Do you know a Samuel?

The woman's mouth had parted, and she snapped it closed. "I do."

Grace nodded and turned her attention back to the man to decipher what the man was showing her. "Ah." Grace smiled. "He was your dad. I see things in terms of a home movie. Sometimes they just give me symbols and sometimes complete pictures. Every now and then they'll talk to me. But your dad showed me you as a little girl, and he was pushing you on a tree swing. You were a cute kid."

"He used to do that a lot when I was young," she answered.

"Perfect." Grace glanced up at the apparition. He held up a coin and flipped it.

"He just flipped a coin and held it up. Both sides are heads. Is that significant for you?"

A tear trickled down Annalise's cheek as she laughed. "That's funny. He used that coin to make me think that it was fate calling the shots. It wasn't until I was older that he came clean and told me he'd just worded the questions for the outcome he thought was in my best interest and then would flip the coin. There was no arguing with the coin when he'd do it several times in a row to make his point."

"Sneaky." Grace grinned and smiled at the apparition. "I like him."

"He would have liked you too," Annalise said at the same time Sam's Aunt Annie appeared.

Grace's brows dipped in confusion as she looked between both women, they shared the same cheek bones, the same styled hair, the same smile and the same looking necklace. "If Annie is your sister, that means you're—"

"Mom," Sam said from behind. "We weren't expecting you for a few more days."

"I came in early, dear," she said, rising and letting Sam kiss her cheeks. "I'm glad I did. I was just having a wonderful chat with your date, Grace."

Grace's mouth parted as words escaped her. She snapped her mouth closed and rose. "The apple doesn't fall far from the tree." Grace picked up her empty wine glass. "I bet if Sam hadn't shown up, you would have pulled out the coin."

Annalise outright laughed. "No need, dear. You've told me everything I need to know." Annalise glanced at Sam. "I like her, Sammy. When are you marrying this one?"

Grace stepped back quickly, knocking over her chair. "Mrs. Stone, it's not like that. I'm sorry if I gave you that impression."

"Oh, you didn't, dear. I have a sense about things," she said as Sam righted the fallen chair.

"I understand why you're here, and I think Sammy was smart for bringing you."

"He didn't really need a date. I have faith he could have handled it."

"I didn't say a date, dear. I said he was smart to bring you."

Grace's cheeks heated as she gave Sam that I'm-sorry look. Grace had fallen for this woman, thinking she was just a hotel guest trying to get out of the heat. She'd told her things, including why she was here. Annalise was one to watch out for. The woman seemed to have a secret agenda and a way of making everyone spill their secrets. Or it might have been the third margarita that had loosened Grace's lips. No, she was sticking with the secret sucking powers that Sam's mother wielded. No one could prove it wasn't so.

Grace smacked Sam in the abs. "No need for a story." She glanced up at him and smiled. "She already knows the truth."

Sam's eyes widened as Grace picked up Annalise's drink, along with her own glass. "Let me get you a refill."

"Don't worry, dear. It's our little secret." Annalise winked at them both before Grace hurried off in hopes of getting

Sam's mother completely drunk so she'd forget everything she'd heard.

Chapter 11

"I leave you alone for a few hours and you confess everything to my mother," Sam hollered into the bathroom where Grace was getting ready for their night out. He continued to pace the hotel room and squeezed his neck. At least he wouldn't have to pretend around his mom. Not that they were doing much pretending anymore. He could see himself and Grace as a couple. He silently wondered if she could too.

"She was hot and wanted to sit in the shade. What was I supposed to do, tell the woman no? I'm not like your ex. Rude and disrespectful doesn't come natural to me, and she didn't introduce herself as your mom. I have to admit, I didn't expect to tell her my life story. She's got that motherly personality that makes a person want to confess everything."

"Of course I didn't want you to be rude," Sam said and turned toward the bathroom door as it opened. Grace stepped out. Her dark hair was curled in a sultry pile on her head. The black silk dress landed mid-thigh and showed a good amount of cleavage...but it was the boots, more specifically, visions of her naked wearing nothing but the boots that made him downright hard. The cowboy boots made her look...local. Every cowboy's wet dream. "Where did you get those boots?"

"The dress shop in the lobby." Grace twisted in place. "Do you like? I should wear my new hat, but they don't really go with my dress."

"Those scream fuck me."

Grace wiggled her brows. "Then they're working and I should buy an extra pair."

Grace twirled, giving Sam a look at the back of her dress. He swallowed around the lump in his throat when he noticed the dip in the back of the dress that landed just above her ass. A silver chain lay down her bare spine. Sam crossed the room and rested his hands on her arms.

"The strippers aren't going to stand a chance with you in the room."

"Is the dress too much?"

"God no." He shook his head. "Although I'm going to have to fight some of the groomsmen. Someone's going to have a black eye in the wedding pictures."

"Oh, you're the psychic now, are you? What else do you see?"

"Me, undressing you, slowly, and figuring out exactly how that necklace is attached."

Grace laughed. "If you're good, I'll show you."

"And if I'm bad?"

"Then you'll see for yourself."

Sam lowered his lips to her shoulder and pressed a sensual kiss on her creamy skin. He didn't want to stop there, but he knew once he got her undressed, he'd never want to leave the room. "I should have done that the day you walked into my office."

"No." Grace ran her fingers up behind his neck. "You should have done this."

Grace lowered his head and met his lips in a special kiss that wasn't meant for anyone else's eyes. Just them. Her tongue dueled in a sensual dance. Her hands clutched his neck as he drank her in. Taking and tasting and enjoying the fact that they didn't have an audience. This was only for them. He could get lost in her taste. The way her soft curves pressed against his body. One hand rested on her hip as he moved the other to touch the bare skin of her back.

There was no hiding his desire. The bulge in his dress pants was evident. He wanted her, and if people weren't waiting on them, he might have talked her into staying in the room the rest of the night and exploring exactly what made her tick. He slowed the kiss, nibbling on her bottom lip as he opened his eyes. Heat and humor sparkled in her eyes. A unique combination that was completely Grace.

"Kissing clients is bad for business."

"I'm not a client." She smiled brightly and stepped out of his hold to grab her purse. "I'm just a girl who thinks you're cute."

"Cute," Sam asked, holding an invisible knife to his chest. "Kids are cute. First crushes are cute. I'm not cute."

"Handsome?" she asked, trying to hold back her smile.

"If you were my mom, maybe, but you wouldn't be kissing me."

"Ah." She nodded in understanding. "Sexy, doable... sausage? Am I getting closer?"

"Yep. Just consider me your personal smorgasbord of meat." He linked their hands and led her out of the hotel room. If he'd kept her in there any longer, they might not leave.

****

The draw of the country music drifted out into the busy parking lot. The neon green sign of a cowgirl leaning on a post lit the night sky. Sam had grown up around the cowboy hat and boot wearing good ole country boy crowd. They worked hard and played harder.

"I thought you said we were going to a strip club," Grace whispered as Sam led her toward the door.

"We are, but Sarah insisted Richard dance with her first. So, we're here for an hour or two before we can ditch her."

"I'm going to need a stiff drink or two if you don't want the bride to have black eyes in the pictures tomorrow. I don't think I'll ever understand what you saw in her."

"I'm beginning to wonder myself."

"First round is on me. We'll toast to you dodging the bullet and to your brother's bad luck."

Sam's smile grew by the minute. Bringing Grace as his date had been a stroke of genius. She was funny and feisty. Her beauty was just a bonus.

Grace walked into the bar as if she'd grown up in this town and everyone knew her name. There wasn't a person she'd met yet she hadn't made to feel comfortable in some way or another, except the bride, of course.

Sam watched Grace as she moved through the crowd and straight to the bar. She wasn't even aware that the groomsmen were undressing her with their eyes, or the way the men naturally gravitated toward her, or how the bartender dropped what he was doing just to serve her.

Why was she still single? He'd spent less than a week with her so far, and he could see what a catch she'd be. The thought of dropping the charade to help her find the type of man she wanted weighed heavy on his mind. Here she was helping him, and what was he doing in return? The opposite of helping her. She thought she'd ruin his chance with the bridesmaids when, in reality, he was ruining her chances at finding the right guy. Did that make him selfish? Would she consider letting him really date her instead?

Sam and Grace downed a shot of whiskey before grabbing their beers and heading toward the wedding party. Sarah was sitting in Richard's lap, even as she watched Sam approach. He'd seen that look in her eyes before. The kind where the claws were itching below the surface. Her gaze was predatory.

Sarah smirked before she turned in Richard's arms and pressed her lips to his in a heated kiss. He'd expected that jab to hurt, but he felt nothing. No hatred or anger or jealousy. Just...nothing. Interesting.

Sam pulled out Grace's chair and took the one next to her. He laid his hand along the back of the chair and took a sip of his beer, doing his best to look happy for his brother.

"So, Sam, how did you two meet?" Sarah asked, as if she was genuinely interested.

Grace raised her brow, as if she was interested in knowing herself. He lifted her hand to his lips and placed a gentle kiss on her knuckles. "She works in the office building directly across from mine, and I asked her out."

"I thought you were going to say she'd come to your office in need of your services helping her find a date," Sarah said with a challenging look.

No one knew that was exactly what had happened.

"Does she look like she needs help finding a date?" Sam asked, raising a brow.

"Hell no," Mike answered. "Grace, do you have any single sisters?"

Grace smiled. "As a matter of fact, one is still single."

"Perfect." Mike rose and held out his hand when a slow song started to play. "Come dance with me and tell me all about her."

Grace rose from her seat and kissed Sam on the lips in a slow, tantalizing kiss that was more heated than the one Sarah had given her groom. "You okay with this?"

"Of course." Sam gave a slow nod. "I trust you explicitly." He said it loud enough for Sarah to hear. His words earned him a bright smile from Grace.

He watched Grace and Mike on the dance floor, unable to look away. Grace spoke as she swayed. She laughed at something Mike said, and Sam forced himself not to cut in. He was watching her for the first time with another man. She seemed confident and in control. The way she smiled and her eyes sparkled held her dance partner a bit mesmerized. Other bridesmaids and groomsmen took to the floor as Richard walked to the bar to get Sarah a drink. She moved into Grace's empty chair.

"You look like you're ready to devour her. You never used to look at me that way. If you had, I might not have found comfort with your brother."

"Yes, you would have. If you'll excuse me." Sam rose from his chair with his gaze locked with Grace's. She licked her lips and winked. More than enough of an invitation for Sam to cut in.

The crowd and people between them parted as if they, too, could feel the building heat that was stirring between Grace and him. With every turn, Grace found his gaze. The look in her eyes turned downright hungry until Sam tapped Mike on the shoulder.

"My turn."

Mike frowned. Yeah, Sam knew why. He finally understood what Grace had meant when she said she wanted the heated gaze from across the room. Sam took her into his arms and twirled her once before pulling her tight against his chest. His lips hovered near her ear, his words a whisper. "Did you feel the heated gaze?"

Goosebumps rose on her arms, telling him what her words didn't.

"What about the butterflies? Are you feeling those yet?"

She leaned out of his hold to glance up at him. "And the pitter-patter," she said as though confused. "It wasn't supposed to happen with you."

Sam rested his fingers in her hair and pulled her flush with his body. "I'm exactly the person you were supposed to experience it with."

He kissed her like a man claiming the last kiss before being shipped off to war. Only things weren't about to end. They were just beginning.

She broke free and shook her head.

"I don't want to help you find another guy," he said, feeling that she was about to run scared.

"Sam—"

He cut her off by kissing her again. The slow sway of their bodies stopped as he broke the kiss and leaned in to whisper in her ear. "Let me date you, for real, Grace."

"I can't." She took his hand and pulled him from the dance floor and out the front door of the bar. She waited until they were on the side of the building before she explained. "I'm not on a rebound and don't need help finding a date. You were right to question the real reason I was in your office. I'm not your typical client."

Sam maneuvered her until her back was pressed against the wall. He lowered his lips to the creamy length of her neck and kissed a path up to her ear. "I know," he whispered between kisses.

"No, you don't," she said, trying to move him away.

"Yes, I do." He leaned back to look into her eyes. "If I tell you the real reason you were in my office, will you let me date you?"

"You can't possibly know."

He went back to kissing her neck on the other side, starting where her neck met her shoulder. His hands slowly moved up her sides. "Chloe McKenzie is your best friend, and my competition."

Her body went rigid beneath his touch, but that didn't deter him. "It's only natural we do background checks on our clients to make sure we don't have any psychos or stalkers. She's your best friend. You were checking out the competition, although you haven't been on a date in a while. My detective was pretty clear that you weren't even looking."

"How did he know?" she asked, leaning her head against the building, giving Sam better access to continue his assault.

"Good-looking men would try to talk to you, and you weren't interested. Men would try and catch your gaze, and you never took the bait. You have a focused life. Work, family, and friends."

"You think you know me?" she asked on a moan as his lips sucked on her ear.

"I don't think, Grace. I know. So, tell me I'm right so we can move past that."

"You knew this whole time and didn't say anything?" she asked, resting her hand on his chest to stop his advances.

Just that slight touch was enough to send his heart racing. Everything about her was enough to bring him to his knees, and he would gladly worship at her feet. His lips and hands wanted to caress every inch of her.

He stopped kissing her long enough to answer. "What kind of matchmaker would I be if I couldn't read people?"

"Your mom overheard my conversation."

"Yes, but I'd already figured it out, and besides, she likes you."

"You aren't mad that I pretended to be a client?"

"I knew it." The familiar voice came from the corner of the building. The bride stood with her arms crossed over her chest. "Your relationship is fake. Why did you bring her, Sam?"

"She's not a client. She's my new—"

"Uh-uh," Grace said, cutting him off. "He doesn't have to explain anything to you. Let me clue you in, Sarah. He's here for his brother, not out of some misguided illusion that you think he's still got a thing for you. Trust me...he doesn't."

"What's going on?" Richard asked as he and the others rounded the building.

"She's horrible," Sarah said as she stormed off with her bridesmaids following behind her.

"What happened?" Richard asked, his gaze questioning as he stared between Sam and Grace.

"Your soon-to-be bride doesn't like my choice of dates," Sam said as he took Grace's hand. "Don't ask me to choose, Richard. You won't like my answer."

"Fair enough. I deserve that."

"Lighten up, people. There's nothing a little bit more alcohol can't cure. Besides, we've got strippers waiting to give a certain groom a lap dance," Stan, one of the groomsmen, added with a playful grin.

Chapter 12

Grace slid into the SUV while debating on calling it a night and letting Sam enjoy time with his brothers and the other guys. He didn't need her with him. There wouldn't be any other women that she needed to keep away from Sam, except maybe a stripper or two, and Sam was capable of thwarting advances.

Her phone rang, and she slipped it out of her purse and glanced at the caller ID to find Aunt Betty calling. She never called unless she'd had a vision or someone was in trouble. Grace answered and pressed the phone to her ear, holding her breath that the apocalypse wasn't upon them.

"Hey, Aunt Betty. You better not be calling me with bad news."

"Actually, I'm calling to tell you that the jet is at the airport for whenever you're ready to leave," Betty said against the sounds of the bar in the background.

"I didn't ask for the jet. Sam has his, and how in the world do you know where I am?" Grace asked, ignoring Sam's questioning looks.

"You're going to need it, doll. Trust me."

Grace turned her gaze to the passing fields and lowered her voice. "What aren't you telling me?"

"I can't say. Your sisters made me promise. But we both know I don't take orders from anyone. You should leave now. Make him take you to the airport. Hell, bring him back with you. Nothing good is going to come out of you staying in Texas for another minute."

"Aunt Betty, just tell me what you saw." Grace knocked Sam's arm. "Stop the car. I need a minute."

Sam pulled over to the shoulder, and Grace jumped out of the SUV and started pacing. "Start talking."

"Sam is going to get hurt, and if you stay, so are you."

Her words had Grace stopping in her tracks. "Like our hearts broken or physically hurt? Which are you talking about?"

"Both. So just get on the plane, Grace. I promised your momma that I wouldn't let you girls get hurt again after what happened with Cara. So, get on the damn plane, Grace."

Grace turned toward the SUV and met Sam's questioning gaze.

"I can't, Aunt Betty. I have to see this through. Deep down in my gut, call it my intuition or whatever you want, I know I have to see this through. My future depends on it."

Aunt Betty's voice turned serious. "You won't have a future if you aren't careful, Grace."

"And Sam? What happens to him if he stays?"

"Grace, do you have wax buildup in your ears? Let me be perfectly clear. If Sam and you stay, one or both of you are going to the hospital with a gunshot wound. Get the hell out of that godforsaken town, or I'm calling in my favors and sending an agent with the FBI to escort your stubborn ass back home."

"How long do I have?"

"You need to be gone before the sun rises."

"His brother is getting married. Sam isn't going to leave," Grace said to placate her aunt. "But I'll work on him."

Grace hung up and spun back to the SUV to find Sam leaning against the passenger door. "Everything okay?"

"No." Grace shook her head. "What kind of chance do I have of getting you to leave Texas with me tonight?"

"Why? What's wrong?"

"That was my Aunt Betty. There's no easy way to tell you this, but we're in danger."

"What kind of danger?"

"The kind you don't walk away from. She wants us to leave."

"I'm the best man. I can't just leave."

"I know." She clasped her hands together. "I'm sorry."

Sam ran his hand through his hair and opened the passenger door. "I can't go, but you should. I'll have my jet fly you home tomorrow and come back for me at the end of the week, after the wedding. You shouldn't stay."

"No need. My company jet was already sent to bring me home. I'll have the pilot waiting for when I'm ready to go. Is there anything I can do to change your mind about leaving with me?" Grace slid up to him and rested her hand on his chest. "Anything at all?"

Sam cupped her neck and pressed his lips to hers. "No, but if your aunt is correct, we might as well make better use of our time."

"I couldn't agree more. How about we go to the club to tell the others we aren't staying and go back to the hotel." Where you'll be safe behind closed doors. She kept that part to herself while she kissed him once more before climbing into the SUV. She could find ways and things for them to do that kept Sam busy and out of the line of fire until the wedding. At least that was her plan, until she had to leave at the last minute.

Sam drove to the strip club where the other SUVs were already parked. The parking lot held only a few cars and a few motorcycles. It was still early, and they weren't busy yet.

They both walked in and headed to the bar for a beer after deciding to have one drink before putting on the show that they couldn't keep their hands off of each other in a plausible excuse for them to leave. She could sell it.

Music blared as lights flashed. Half-clad women were on the stage, twirling around the pole and dancing provocatively. Men wearing everything from leather vests to business suits sat around the stage and in the darkened corners, where a few were in the process of getting lap dances. Some of the men were drinking, some just watching like voyeurs. A few guys in cowboy hats lined the bar, and Grace immediately recognized them from the grounds around the hotel she'd seen while on her jog and in the pool.

Michael, Stan, and Richard had a booth near the stage. Stan was in the process of shoving some dollars in the woman's thong. Sam kept his arm around Grace's shoulder or on her back as if he was staking his claim for all others to see. Grace didn't mind. They wouldn't be in the bar long enough for anything to happen. Not if she had her way. She needed time to talk to Aunt Betty again and grill her sisters for a bit more specific information about the shooter, like when and where or even name and room number would have been helpful.

Sam kissed her neck and whispered into her ear, "Ten minutes max and we're out of here."

Grace nodded and danced toward the bachelor party table. The men were wearing big, bright smiles. They had a table full of shots lined up. Stan handed Grace and Sam one as they approached. "You guys need to catch up."

Sam set his down. "I'm driving."

"Aw, man, don't be a party pooper. We can call you a cab."

"I'll drive." Grace handed her shot to Sam. "You should have a shot with your brother. Make memories since we won't be staying long," she said with a smile and took a seat at one of the dark booths behind the table and out of the way. She really didn't want to be the cause of him not enjoying this special time with his brother, even if neither Sam nor she liked the bride.

Grace sat at the table while Sam handed his brother a few shots and patted him on the back. She couldn't hear their words, not that it mattered. A waitress showed up with a beer on her tray and set it down in front of Grace. "It's from the cowboy at the bar."

Grace nodded. "Tell him thanks, but I don't need anymore. I'm driving. Do you mind bringing me a bottled water?"

"Sure thing, hun."

"Thanks."

The waitress returned and placed the bottled water on the table along with a slip of paper with a phone number on it. Grace's brows dipped. "The cowboy in the black hat."

Grace glanced to the guy at the bar. His belt buckle was almost as big as his head. He tipped his hat in way of greeting, and Grace gave him a quick smile of thanks before turning back to find Richard handing Sam something. Sam's heated gaze was on Grace. She could feel the flames coursing through her body. Within seconds Sam was by her side and sitting at the table, his arm around the back of the booth.

"I don't think you realize how many men admire you."

"Black Cowboy Hat sent over his number." Grace grinned.

"You won't need it," Sam said, taking a sip of his still half-full beer. "You promised to let me date you if I guessed why you were in my office."

"Ah." She nodded. "I almost forgot." As if. She slid onto his lap and straddled him. Her dress was hiked up to her thighs, and the only things separating her heat and his bulge were her panties and his jeans. She wrapped her hands around his neck. "Ready to leave?"

His hands slipped beneath her dress and landed on her ass. "Thong?" He grinned. "My favorite."

She nodded, and he squeezed her ass cheeks, shooting a bit of excitement up her spine.

"Kiss me and mean it," she demanded.

He leaned closer to her and kissed the swells of her breasts, which were peeking out from her dress. He kissed a path up her neck as he held her bottom against him, stopping her squirm.

His lips tilted up into a lazy smile as he met her gaze. "You like that?"

"I like a lot of things." Her heart raced against her ribcage as his hands toyed with the scrap of material going down her crack. He leaned forward and kissed her hard. He took what she gave, wanting, craving more, bringing every one of her nerve endings to life in a lust filled haze. "You should tell them bye."

He rose, slowly letting her slide down his body. "I already did."

He lowered her dress down her thighs. Each agonizing inch against her sensitive skin ensured that she wasn't leaving Texas without taking him for a trial run, or two, during a hot unadulterated sex-a-thon. Feeling his need and desire for her, for the first time in a long time, she'd truly felt wanted and needed. He'd given her back what she thought was unattainable, that elusive partner she thought didn't exist, and she wasn't ready to walk away. Not yet.

He took her by the hand and led her outside. She'd follow him just to see if what he promised was just as good as the real thing. What started as a game had the possibility to be so much more. Her panties were wet in anticipation. His erection bulged behind his zipper. They were both in need of a cold shower, if they planned to keep their wits about them.

"I hope you're ready for a long hot ride, Ms. Thatcher."

She was and she knew they'd never make it back to the hotel room before one or both of them found release. It was just a matter of whether Sam was going to screw her in the back seat or if he was going to find somewhere else.

"The hotel is too far away," she whispered around his kisses as he backed her up until she was pressed against the door. The smell of his cologne surrounded her, soothed her. Made her forget their problems.

"I know." He rested his forehead against hers and clenched his eyes closed. "I know of a place where it will just be us. No threats, no guests, no hotel workers. Just us, and it's closer."

"Where?" she asked excitedly, trying to calm the rapid beat of her heart.

He slipped his fingers beneath her dress and inched her panties to the side, running the pad of his finger through her wet folds before moving it inside of her hot, wet channel. A moan slipped free as she clenched his arm. The need to keep him inside of her left her frenzied with desire. He pulled it out while holding her gaze, and placing the finger in his mouth, he sucked her desire from the digit before kissing her hard once again. The musky taste of her arousal drove her need only higher.

"I wasn't expecting that," she said, out of breath, fighting the need to ask for more.

"I read it in your book." He winked. "It's not far. Do you trust me?"

"Yes."

Chapter 13

Ten minutes later, Sam drove through an iron gate with a sign above it that read, Stone Ranch. This was the first official ranch that Grace had been to. A white, two-story house with blue shutters and a picket fence sat off in the distance. A thin forest lined one side of the property. On the others, there were just fields of green pasture. She could see for miles in three directions, but not beyond the woods.

"Which Stone lives here?" she asked.

"It's where I grew up. I own it, but Richard runs it with our ranch manager, Steve."

"If he runs it, why is everyone staying at the hotel?"

Sam shrugged. "I'm sure that was more Sarah's idea than Richard's. She's always wanted a lifestyle outside her means."

"Then why didn't she stick with you? I mean, you own your own company."

"Not when we were engaged. I hadn't decided what I wanted to do with my life, up until she broke my heart."

"And so you've made it your personal mission to mend everyone else's?"

"Something like that." Sam bypassed the main house and pulled up behind the barn.

"You can't be suggesting..."

"That's exactly what I'm suggesting. Don't worry. The horses were boarded on a neighbor's ranch and the staff has the week off due to the wedding. It's just us and there's no one to disturb us. No one even knows we're here. The entire place is ours."

"Then why not a bed?" she asked, climbing out.

"Bad memories," he offered as his only clue. He didn't need to say anymore. She knew exactly what he meant. Somewhere up in that house there were memories he'd like to forget. She'd help him make more memories, so that when he returned, he'd have something even better to remember.

"You sure you wouldn't like a nice, comfortable bed? I can help you create new memories."

"Where's your sense of adventure?" He teased before slipping out of the SUV and taking her hand. He led her into the barn and up into a loft type area, which was filled with hay. There was a window on the second story that was partially open. Grace walked to it and glanced down at the pile of hay below. "I bet you jumped from here when you were a kid."

"You know I did." He pulled her to him.

"All you're missing is a cowboy hat, stud, and you could give me the full experience."

"Next time." Sam ran the pad of his thumb down her arm, driving the thrill of her needs to new heights. She was nuts, certifiably so, for not immediately heeding her aunt's demand to leave. There was something about Sam that made her feel welcome, and home, something she couldn't describe, something she didn't want to analyze. She just wanted to experience it right then, with him.

"You have goosebumps," he said before kissing her. He traced a path over her outer thigh and beneath her dress. The feel of his hands on her thong excited her, as did the tear they made when he ripped them free. She had not been expecting that either.

"You read that in my book."

His lips twitched. "Maybe. Let's see if it turned you on."

He ran his finger through her folds and moaned. "Damn, woman. It did."

"I told you...women writers. Men could take a hint."

"You've given me a whole new reason to read." He dropped to his knees in front of her and kissed her inner thigh. The feel of his lips against her skin made her part her legs more. His chuckle filled the open loft as his hands caressed her ass. "I'm going to taste you."

His words sent a ripple of awareness up her spine. The cool evening breeze from the open barn window chilled her sensitive bud making her shiver, and her nipples puckered beneath her dress. He blew on her sex before covering it with his mouth.

Grace cupped his head, holding on to keep herself from flying into orbit. The scent of her arousal permeated the air as he ran his tongue through her folds, tasting and teasing her to the point that her legs were shaking. Her need spiraled out of control until she was on the verge of breaking when he slowly pulled away. He rose and kissed her, taking his time to let her taste herself on his lips.

"I want to taste all of you," he said, turning her.

The sound of her zipper being lowered had moisture forming between her legs. Sam slid the silky material down her arms, letting it pool at her feet around her boots before he reached for the silver chain and ran it through his fingers to her shoulders. Every ounce of her wanted to tell him to turn her to see where it ended, but she didn't.

The slide of his fingers over her shoulders as they followed the delicate chain that split around the neck and descended down the front of her body. He moaned when he found it attached to her nipple piercings.

"You're the definition of sexy," he whispered.

She reached behind her back, and between their bodies, unhooking his jeans and lowering his zipper.

He turned her in his arms and lowered her into the hay. His lips touched and tasted every inch of her exposed skin before he undressed. He rested between her thighs and held her gaze as he positioned himself at her entrance.

"Condom?" she asked, almost afraid that he wouldn't have one. She was on the pill, but one could never be too careful, especially with the way women were turning up pregnant in her family.

Sam slipped a wrapper out of his pocket and ripped it open. The neon yellow glowed.

"Pretty. Just think. We'll be able to find you if you get lost in the dark," she whispered.

"I don't think you'll misplace anything of mine."

His bulge was long and thick. He was most definitely right. "I've seen your goods. Show me you can make neon disappear." She smiled.

"My brother insisted I needed the condom more than he did. He must have known we wouldn't make it back to the hotel."

"Remind me to thank your brother."

She took the condom and rolled it down his shaft. He eased her back and repositioned himself. He held her gaze as he slid inside her tight channel. Sweat beaded on his brow as he took his time, easing into her.

"You won't hurt me," she said and dug her boot heels into his ass. "Take me for a ride, cowboy."

"You've got it, baby."

Sam winked and slid hard into her, stealing her breath. He eased in and out of her, filling her as he set up a pace and a rhythm that was sending her to new heights. She moaned as she dug her nails into his arms, wanting and needing him to feel everything she was.

"You're so tight," he murmured between clenched teeth as he continued his thrust.

"It's been a while," she said, lifting her hips to meet each of his thrusts.

He drove into her, his shaft pulsing with every thrust. She could feel her channel tighten on him and knew she was close. Neither of them would last long, not this first time. And it was definitely the first of many times tonight.

He wrapped his teeth around the nipple ring and gave a little tug, sending a path of electricity straight to her core that sent her flying over the edge. Her muscles tightened around his shaft again as she cried out his name, coaxing his orgasm from him until he was seated deep inside her when he stilled, the muscles of his body hard as he gave a little thrust with another moan.

"Oh God."

He collapsed to his elbows and deeply kissed her, taking his time to appreciate her thoroughly.

"I hope he gave you more than one condom."

He shook his head. "I wasn't expecting this. We'll have to go back to the hotel for more."

Sam rolled off her and pulled her into his side. He moved some of the hay over their bodies, aggravated he hadn't thought to carry a blanket up to the rafters with them.

The creaking sound of a barn door opening made them still. Her eyes bulged as Sam handed her the dress and reached for his jeans. They tried as quietly as they might to redress.

"Sarah, you're running out of time to convince him to sleep with you. He's not going to need to be a math genius to realize this child isn't his," an unfamiliar male voice said.

Grace didn't recognize the male voice and she froze, holding the dress up against her body. Sam's cheeks turned an angry red, and not from the strenuous rafter play. He looked ready to explode as he clenched and unclenched his fists.

Grace grabbed his hand and shook her head, holding her finger over her lips.

"I poked holes in the neon condom and told him I couldn't wait until our wedding day to have sex. That I wanted him tonight. I even paid the guys to make sure he was hot and horny. I'm trying my best to fix this, Steve."

Grace's eyes bulged as her gaze went to the discarded condom. She covered her mouth with her hand. Sam mouthed obscenities that would have made her sister, Quinn, proud. It was something she would have expected from her Aunt Betty. Not Sam's ex, Sarah. Yep, they were screwed...literally. Had this been what Aunt Betty meant when she said their lives were in danger? God forbid one of them has a gun.

Sam's face hardened in anger. He looked on the verge of blowing his lid and getting them both caught. Grace grabbed his arm and shook her head. They peered over the railing to find Steve had Sarah by the throat and pinned to the wall. He kissed her hard. "If he finds out you cheated on him with me, and that I knocked you up, he's not going to marry you. And you know what that means, no wedding, no honeymoon. No honeymoon, no life insurance with you as the beneficiary. There will be no payout on his death on your one-year anniversary. We'll be back to square one with a new kid and no money. We need his fucking money, baby. You need to make him believe that he got you pregnant, and that the baby just came earlier than expected. Everyone else will think you're a helpless widow with a baby. They won't think twice that you fell for your ranch manager. The cops won't suspect a thing."

"I'll fix this. You know I can always seduce Sam and make him responsible. He's still got it bad for me, and he's worth a lot more money than his brother. I should have just stayed with him; we could have finished this years ago and be together by now."

"He'd be harder to kill in Florida. No, we need it to be Richard, and out on the ranch, where there are less prying eyes."

"I know, you're right. I need to get back to the hotel before Sam gets back to find I'm not there since the rest of the girls are already back. I just had to see you one more time."

Sam stumbled back and knocked some hay from the rafters as the couple turned to leave.

Sarah gasped as Steve called out, "Who's up there?"

Grace covered her mouth with her hand, and her body with her clothes she'd yet to fully dress in.

"I heard everything, and you better believe I'm not going to let my brother marry a two-bit whore," Sam said as he walked toward the railing. He held a finger up to his lips to keep Grace quiet.

"Oh my God," Sarah screamed. "You...you...."

"What are you doing out here, Sam?" Steve asked as Grace heard the unmistakable cock of a gun trigger. Sam climbed down the ladder and out of view.

"I had a fight with Grace. She left town, and I came out here for some peace."

"You'll have plenty of that where you're going," Steve said before a shot rang out.

Grace's entire body shook, and her breath caught as fear froze her in place.

"Why'd you go and do that?" Sarah asked. "Now how am I going to explain that his brother went missing from the wedding?"

Sam's moan was the first clue that he wasn't dead. "You'll never get away with it."

"Sure we will. You said it yourself. You came here for peace, to think, and have a few beers. An unexpected robbery and burnt body should do the trick. They'll think the robber shot you and left you inside before setting the barn on fire to cover his tracks. We'll take some things from the house and make it look like you were in the wrong place at the wrong time. They'll never be able to tell the difference with the fire damage."

"Get his wallet and phone, Sarah, and everything that might be worth money, then get out of here. Get back to the hotel so you have an alibi. Make sure plenty of people see you."

"What do you want me to do with his stuff?"

"Put it with his aunt's necklace and the other stuff in the metal tin, by the creek, on your way back to the hotel. They'll never find where it's buried."

"The rock wall. You're a genius." Her words vibrated with enthusiasm.

Enthusiasm that Grace was going to yank from this woman's heart and give to her brother-in-law, Collin's, dog as a chew toy. No way could Grace let this woman marry and kill Sam's brother. It wasn't happening. She just needed to figure out a plan to get Sam and herself out alive before creating voodoo dolls and turning these two into pincushions. Grace shimmied her dress over her head and slid on her boots.

"Why did you steal the necklace?"

"I wanted it." Sarah smirked.

She peered over the ledge and watched as Sarah took Sam's wallet and phone while Steve held the gun on him. "Sarah, you take care of his things while I head to my place to get the kerosene. I'll take care of this asshole once and for all."

Sarah and Steve backed away toward the door and out of the barn. The sound of them shoving something against the door to trap Sam and Grace inside filled the silence. Sam met Grace's gaze as she hurried down from the loft and to his side.

Blood oozed from his chest wound, soaking the fabric of his shirt.

"Tell me what to do," she begged, glancing around the barn for anything they could use.

"There used to be a first aid kit on the wall. You need to try and patch me up so we can get out of here. I'm sure we don't have much time before he torches the place." Sam laid back and held his hand over the wound.

Grace ran to where Sam gestured, grabbed the box, and slid back down beside him. She hurried and used all of the gauze and everything in the box to help stop the bleeding. A doctor she wasn't, but damn, if her momma hadn't taught her how to stuff a turkey.

"He locked us in, Grace. We're going to need to find another way out."

Grace quickly glanced around the area. There were no windows, no doors other than the one they'd entered, and not even any rotten wood that she could try and pull away. Her gaze landed on the little bit of moonlight that was illuminating the dirt floor. She followed the beam to the rafters.

"I know what to do."

She hurried up the stairs to the rafters and to the window in time to see Steve pulling a knife out of Sam's tire and climbing into a dusty truck to drive away.

"He stabbed your tires," she yelled below.

"Crap," she heard him exclaim.

Grace walked to the opening and glanced down to the ground. A pile of hay was stacked below. "Hang on, Sam. I can get us out." She lowered her voice and mumbled, "If I don't break my neck. This is going to hurt."

"What are you doing?" Sam hollered.

"Jumping."

"Have you lost your mind?" he asked.

"I'm so not dressed for this," she whispered and didn't offer him an explanation as she sat down at the window with her legs dangling out. Using the traction of her boots, she eased herself out of the opening and slowly lowered herself out the window using her feet as if she were a rock climber.

"Just like Spidey," she whispered to herself. "Although hand suction would be useful." The muscles in her arms burned as she tried to hold her weight, thankful for her years as a gymnast. She glanced down at the drop below. She could nail this landing. She'd done it from high beams while flipping in the air, and this was a straight drop.

She took a deep breath and let go, relaxing her muscles to roll when her feet touched the ground. She lay still on the mound, looking up at the stars in the night sky. She'd survived, even if the hay scratched and poked in places that hadn't seen daylight in years. It was still a win, and she'd take it.

She rolled off the hay until she was standing and hurried around the building. She struggled to move the big board holding the doors closed. Eventually she managed to pull it free and open the door. She hurried inside to help Sam to stand.

"You jumped from the window?" he asked as he pulled a few pieces of hay from her hair.

"Piece of cake. I was a gymnast, remember?"

"Thank God for that," he said as she moved his good arm over her shoulder to give him some leverage to help him walk.

"How are we going to get help?"

"The neighbor is a doctor. His place is just past the creek. We just need to get to him," Sam said, gesturing toward the woods.

"Remind me to wear jeans and tennis shoes next time we go out."

"It could be worse. You could be wearing heels."

Grace rolled her eyes. "Says the man bleeding to death."

Chapter 14

The creek was only half a mile away and was the dividing line between the properties. Sam could feel his energy draining with each step. He could no longer hide the grimace from his face or prevent the groans from slipping free. He wasn't going to make it to the neighbor's house.

"I need to rest," he said, sliding down the stone wall. His stuff was hidden around there somewhere, but he didn't have the energy to look. He needed Grace to run, and keep running, until she was safe. "My stuff should be around here somewhere, but we don't have time to look. You need to go."

"Don't you mean we," she begged. "He could have already come back and realized you're gone."

"I can't." He lifted his hand and dropped it again. "You go." He pointed. "His place is a half a mile through the field. Either the doctor or his daughter will probably spot you coming."

"I can't leave you," Grace said, dropping to her knees. She rested her scratched-up palm on his face.

He covered her palm with his. "I bet this wasn't exactly the vacation you had in mind."

"Oh, I don't know. I'd say this wedding is one I won't soon forget, considering you probably knocked me up. I'm sure I'll remember it for the rest of my life." She smiled as a tear trickled over her cheek. She was trying to be strong for both of them.

A laugh bubbled free, and he regretted the small movement. His entire body was starting to go lax. The fight in him was dying as the need to close his eyes was close to winning.

"Grace, you need to go." He turned his face and kissed her palm. "For our future baby's sake." He smiled, knowing he'd probably never get the chance to say those words again.

"Look who's got a sense of humor in the face of death." She rose. "I'm going to kill your ex. You won't have to worry about her marrying your brother." She glanced over her shoulder, back in the direction of the barn, and then toward the doctor's house. She squatted in front of him. "Don't die on me. You owe me a real date."

"Go, Grace."

She nodded and took off in a jog, going only a few steps before she stopped and ditched the boots on her feet. She glanced back and grinned before she took off at a faster pace toward the doctor's house.

Sam strained to keep his eyes open until she made it out of sight. Only after knowing she was far enough out of harm's way did he let his body succumb to the pain and blood loss. He closed his eyes in the silence and let himself slip further into the awaiting darkness.

****

Grace sat in the chair across the room from where Sam was resting. Doctor Halloway had performed a miracle, and removed the bullet lodged in Sam's chest, in his home clinic. Thank God for small miracles. Sam had an IV in his arm and a bandage across his bare chest. Color had started returning to his cheeks, but he still looked worse than her sisters after a night out on the town. The sound of the heart rate monitor was her only company in the silence of the room. Sam had barely had a pulse by the time she'd gotten back to him.

"He's going to be fine." Rose, Doc Halloway's daughter, said from the doorway. "He'll recover. My dad got to him in time."

"I know."

Rose walked into the room and handed Grace a towel, a pile of clothes, and a pair of sneakers. "I thought you might like to take a shower and change."

"Thank you." Grace took them but didn't walk out. "That guy, Steve, is going to come here looking for Sam. How long until he wakes up?"

Rose let out a long sigh. "I'm not sure, but don't worry about Steve. We have ranch hands; my dad has guns, and we've called the law to have Steve arrested."

Grace smiled. "Excellent. I have a wedding to stop."

****

Grace tossed the doors open to the private dining area where the rehearsal dinner was being held. All eyes turned in her direction at the noise. Grace scanned the occupants until she found the woman that was enjoying her last meal as a free woman.

"Thank goodness you made it," Annalise said as she rose from the table and met Grace in the middle of the room. "Where's Sam?"

"I'll get to that," Grace said, patting Annalise's hand before moving inside the room.

The table was set up in a U-shape, the bride and groom in the center with the rest of the wedding party on both sides. Sam's chair next to his brother was empty.

Grace walked over to the table and tossed a neon-colored condom packet onto the bride's plate and smirked. "Sorry to disappoint your plans."

Grace glanced at Richard, who looked like a little-lost boy. "She's pregnant, and the baby isn't yours. It belongs to your ranch manager, Steve."

"That's a lie," Sarah yelled and rose.

"She put holes in the condom that you gave your brother last night. She wanted you to think that you were the one who got her pregnant."

Sarah's mouth parted as the blood drained from her face. "She's lying."

"Afraid not." Grace tossed a metal box onto the table with cash, jewels and Sam's wallet and phone inside. Where the rest of the jewelry and cash had come from she didn't have a clue, but she knew exactly who'd stolen it. "She planned to kill you on your one year anniversary, for the money."

"I would never." Sarah raised a hand to her chest as if Grace had stabbed her in the heart with a knife. There was still a possibility.

"What did you do?" Richard asked, rising. His voice grew deeper with each syllable.

"It's worse," Grace added. "She was with Steve when he shot your brother in the barn. They left him for dead after telling him their plan for Sarah to trick you into marrying her, and how Steve was going to kill you. They didn't know I was there. I witnessed the entire thing."

"Oh my God," Annalise shrieked. "Where's Sam?"

Grace glanced over her shoulder. "He's fine. I got us out of the barn and found help. He's recovering."

Sarah started inching around the table, as if she was going to run, and the entire wedding party was just watching her make her way to the door when the police stepped into view, stopping her advance.

"Sarah Singletary, you're under arrest for attempted murder and conspiracy to commit murder. You have the right to remain silent."

"I'll kill you," she shrieked and broke free, making a beeline straight for Grace, but she was stopped short by Annalise, who stepped in front of Sarah and punched her in the nose.

The police grabbed Sarah, and this time, put her in cuffs and led her from the room.

Richard plopped down in his chair and dropped his gaze. His world had crumbled in the blink of an eye. The betrayal wouldn't be easy to swallow. Seconds ticked by in the silent room. No one spoke; no one dared. Richard raised his gaze to Grace.

"Where's my brother?"

"Doc Halloway's house."

Annalise grabbed Grace's hand and followed Richard from the room and out of the hotel. The ride back to the doctor's home was made in silence. Two men stood on the porch wearing cowboy hats and brandishing shotguns, as if on a lookout in the Wild West. Grace would have taken a picture for Aunt Betty if the situation hadn't been so dire.

Doc Halloway walked out onto the porch along with Rose, each carrying weapons aimed at the car. It wasn't until Annalise, Richard, and Grace stepped out that everyone let down their guard.

Annalise and Richard hurried inside, following behind Rose. Grace stopped in front of the doc.

"Has he woken yet?"

"Yes, about five minutes after you left. He's been asking for you, and he wasn't happy when I told him that you'd gone to stop the wedding, until I told him you'd gone to the police station first."

"Thank you for helping us and for what you did for him." Grace kissed the old man's cheek. "I don't know how I can repay you."

"I've had this property since his grandparents owned the ranch. They've helped me more times than I care to admit. They're good people."

"I know."

"Grace," Annalise said as she poked her head outside the door. "Sam wants to see you."

"Thanks again, Doc." Grace squeezed his arm as she passed and followed Sam's mom into the house. Richard was sitting next to the bed with his head in his hands as Grace entered the room. There weren't any words that would ever suffice at making things right again after what had happened.

"I'm so sorry," Richard repeated over and over again.

"You dodged a bullet," Sam said, cupping the back of Richard's neck.

"You didn't," Richard said, glancing up at his brother with tears in his eyes.

Annalise cleared her throat, and the guys looked in her direction. There was an awkwardness that hadn't been there before. Maybe it had to do with the fact that Grace was responsible for breaking the news, maybe not. "Richard, let's give them a minute."

"We'll just be outside. I'll make arrangements to get you airlifted to the hospital and have you checked out." Richard glanced in her direction. "I can make sure you get back to Florida."

"No need. I'm a big girl. My jet is at the airport and ready to fly whenever I am, but thank you." Grace squeezed Richard's arm in passing before he walked out, shutting the door behind him.

"Hey you." Grace smiled as she approached the bed.

"I'm the worst date ever." He grinned.

"Believe it or not, I've had worse." She winked and sat on the bed next to him. She wrapped her hand around his and linked their fingers. "Thanks for not dying on me. That would have really sucked."

Sam shrugged. "Oh, I don't know. I still would have haunted you. I could have given you dating tips in ghost form."

Grace chuckled. "Yes, you could have, but you're forgetting I'm not a client."

"You're right. You're not a client; you're my hero."

"That's me." Grace smiled. "Able to leap from tall buildings in a single bound, or just fall from second-story barns and not break my neck. Same thing. I just need to get you one of those call signals made that I can see in the night sky."

"Save your money. I'll just flash the lights in my office to get your attention."

"Steve and Sarah have been arrested, and I've already given my statement to the police."

"Good." Sam rested his hand on her flat stomach. "How's our baby?"

"Non-existent." Grace slipped off the bed and kissed his lips. "The condom was a second layer of protection. I'm on the pill, so barring I'm one of the two-percenters...we should be good."

Richard poked his head into the room, halting their conversation. "The helicopter should be here in five minutes."

"Thanks," Sam said and turned his loving gaze to Grace. "Are you going to stay?"

"I'm going to fly home and get out of everyone's hair. I think this couch potato has had enough excitement. Are you going to be good?"

"I'll be fine, thanks to you."

"Yeah. What can I say? I saved you from the bridesmaids and from bleeding out. Where would you be without me?"

"Where indeed?"

"So I guess I'll see you when I see you." Grace leaned over and pressed her lips to his for possibly the last time. Her heart clenched at the thought.

"You can count on it."

The sound of the whipping blades on the chopper outside the window drowned out whatever else Sam was about to say. Grace moved to the window and watched the paramedics in flight suits push a stretcher through the yard. "Looks like your chariot awaits."

The door opened and the room turned into a frenzy of activity, with the paramedics trying to get Sam onto the stretcher and Sam's family members trying to help while asking questions.

The entire Stone family left in the helicopter, leaving Grace behind. Not that she minded. They were his family. They needed to be with him.

"Can I give you a lift back to the hotel and to the airport?" Rose asked.

"That would be great."

The windows were down in the truck. The incoming breeze from the evening wind caressed Grace's face.

She was alive. They were both alive.

A tear formed behind her eyes. It was the first time since the barn that she allowed herself to feel the impact of what had just happened. She'd found the most incredible man and had nearly lost him forever. Even if they never dated, just knowing he was alive would be enough.

"Don't worry. Dad said he'll be fine," Rose said reassuringly.

"I almost lost him before I even had him. I don't know what's wrong with me. I'm not a crier." Grace rested a hand over her stomach to calm her raging butterflies.

"When we care about someone, we all turn a little crazy. I won't tell anyone you shed a few tears."

Chapter 15

Grace dragged her suitcase behind her into the house and dropped her keys on the table in the foyer. She was finally home. The flight back had been smooth and without incident. She ignored the gazillion texts and messages that her family had been leaving for her, popping off a single text to Aunt Betty that she was fine and to spread the word. Grace was too tired to deal with visitors. Her bed was calling and she planned to sleep like a baby for the remainder of her time off.

A week later, when the wine was gone, and her books were read, she was standing at her office window staring at

Sam's dark office across the street. She hadn't heard from him. She didn't even know if he'd returned or if they'd found any complications. Heck, she didn't even have a way to get ahold of his family to find out how he was doing. An empty feeling settled into the pit of her stomach. The phone on her desk rang, pulling her from her thoughts. She answered it.

"This is Grace."

"Tell me you learned all of his secrets," Grace's best friend, Chloe, cooed into the phone.

"Hardly, but I'm pretty sure I learned everything not to do on a wedding date if that helps."

"So, how was it? How was he? Minus the whole getting shot thing and murder plot?"

"Someone in my family has a big mouth."

"Of course they do. I might have run into your aunt, and she spilled the beans. I'm surprised you didn't call me."

"Sorry. I've been busy." Busy doing nothing but avoiding having to answer questions that she still hadn't figured out.

Chloe laughed. "Do you still think he's awful?"

"The worst, if you mean as in a sexy, good-looking guy that has an exceptional personality, along with stamina."

"Men with stamina are keepers," Quinn said as she entered the office, holding her palm over her pregnant belly.

"Listen, Chloe. I've got to go. Quinn is eavesdropping again."

"No problem. I'll just be here, trying to figure out how in the hell I'm going to pay my bills and save my company."

"I'll help you figure it out, but I've got to go. Quinn is making a weird scrunching face while holding her belly."

"Oww." Quinn let out an earth-shattering screech and took several Lamaze-type breaths. "Fuck me," she said between pants. "Get my ass to a hospital before this child splits me in two."

Grace slammed down the office phone, took Quinn by the arm, and led her out of the office. "Don't be breaking your water all over my office. Find a cork and plug that sucker up."

Grace called out through the office to anyone in hearing distance. "Someone find my sisters and tell them Quinn's cuss marathon has begun and to call Collin. He had a hand in making her this way. It's only fair he should have to deal with the repercussions."

"Fuck you. Owwww." She screamed again as the elevator doors opened.

"Just breathe, Quinn."

"Bite me." Quinn held on to the elevator railing as they descended, and

Grace fired off a group text to Collin and the entire family, not trusting that anyone heard her demands over Quinn's outburst of pain.

The elevator dinged, and Cara stood outside the door, a puddle of water at her feet as she held her stomach. This was not happening. Not both sisters at once. Was this karma or payback? "Not you too?"

Cara nodded and started breathing in quick short bursts.

The security guard's eyes bulged as he hurried to the front door, holding it open for them to pass.

Grace unlocked her car and eased both sisters in before climbing behind the wheel and peeling off down the street. There was no way in hell they were having these babies all over her leather seats.

"We're not going to make it," Quinn screamed. "I need drugs. God, someone give me drugs."

"Keep your legs crossed and just breathe, Quinn," Grace demanded.

"If you say that one more time, so help me..."

"Here, squeeze my hand," Cara offered, and the panting continued. Grace started doing it with them, all the way to the hospital, to appease them and stall the next contraction.

"We're here." Grace skidded to a halt outside the hospital's ER.

She ran inside and yelled for help before returning to help both sisters out of the car. When they were settled in wheelchairs and being hauled away, Grace moved her car into a parking spot before sending another text that Cara was also in labor and that they were all at the hospital. God help the hospital staff when all the Thatchers and their spouses converged. Aunt Betty alone was enough to scare off doctors, but throw in a hit man, an ex-FBI agent, and a high-strung Highlander, and the nurses would either be drooling at how good looking the guys were, or would be ready to throw them out when they realized that the Thatcher husbands, combined, had the patience of a toddler being told no while dangling candy in front of him.

Shit was about to get real. Their temperaments were already combustible and explosive. Hide the oxygen tanks and sharp objects. This was going down like the Hindenburg.

Grace stood outside the hospital and debated running away instead of going inside. They knew she was here. There was no escape, no way to play ignorant. Grace walked inside and followed the signs to the maternity ward.

"Cockanoodlemonkeylovingsonofamother."

Grace smiled, hearing Quinn's cussing from down the hall. The new obscenities she was screaming would never be added to dictionaries. She was going to have to record this for future blackmail. Grace stopped at the nurses' desk.

"Which rooms are the Thatcher sisters in?"

"202 and 203."

Great. Right next to each other. "Thanks."

Grace went back and forth from Quinn's room to Cara's, trying her best to give her sisters moral support until Collin and Coop arrived to take over. When she pulled out her phone, to record the moment with her video, she had to dodge water bottles and sharp objects that were being thrown at her head.

Within thirty minutes, Grace was drained of energy, minus feeling in some of her fingers, and had a possible busted eardrum, thanks to a contraction hitting Quinn while Grace was near the bed.

Collin and Coop showed up, passing Grace in the hall. "They're both at six centimeters. Keep the sharp objects out of reach and take some earplugs. You're going to need them," she said, wiping the sweat from her brow. "You two owe me...big....huge."

Collin lifted Grace into a hug and swung her around. "That I do, lass."

"Put me down and go deal with Quinn. God knows the nurses need you in there as a new target."

"Coop, Cara's in the room next door. I'm going to get a coffee and collapse."

"Thanks, Grace." Coop kissed her cheek in passing.

****

Sam leaned against the limo door outside the hospital and debated going inside after just missing Grace as she was leaving her office building with her two very pregnant sisters holding their bellies and doing that crazy Lamaze breathing. He knew exactly where Grace was headed, and the joy and panic that would consume her.

"Are you just going to stand there all day, Sam, or are you going to go upstairs to get a glimpse at how your life is about to change?" a woman said from behind him.

Sam turned to find an older woman with orange spiked hair grinning at him. The shirt she wore read, "Great Aunts are Hot."

"Excuse me? I'm sorry, do I know you?"

"You can call me Aunt Betty. That's what Grace calls me."

"Oh." He nodded slowly in understanding. She was the woman who had foretold their danger at the wedding. "Right. You're the Aunt Betty with the visions."

"One and the same. There's no need to thank me. Maybe just make an altar with my picture as the centerpiece." She entwined their arms together before glancing at the limo driver. "He'll be down in ten with company, so park it, good looking."

"I should probably just leave," he said as she started dragging him inside.

"Nonsense. She's waited long enough to hear from you. You're about to lose your window of opportunity, and we both know you don't want that."

"I'm sure she's busy," Sam said, digging in his heels to make Betty stop.

"Listen, sonny. You have free will, but she does too, and her will is almost ready to knock yours on its ass. So, suck it up and be the man she thinks you are. You promised her a date, and you're the dating king, so give her one that she'll compare all others against."

"See, now that I can do," Sam said, straightening his shirt. "Thanks." He'd turned to walk away when Betty grabbed his arm, stopping his retreat.

"Oh, and one more thing."

Sam raised his brow.

"Don't order any wine or champagne. She can't drink."

Sam crossed his arms over his chest. "Why can't she drink?"

"Because you knocked her up."

"She said she was on the pill."

"She's one of the two-percenters. Congratulations, dad; you're having a girl. I expect her to be named after me."

Sam's mouth parted, and he stood frozen in place as he watched the crazy woman walk away. Sarah's deceit with the condom had screwed them both. "Fuck me," he said to himself, earning him some horrendous stares from women entering the hospital.

"She already did," Betty hollered out.

Sam spun on his heels, intent on heading back to the car while letting Betty's words consume his thoughts. His mind raced, trying to figure out exactly how he was supposed to process that news. It wasn't as if he'd never wanted to get married or have kids, but a baby with Grace, after everything they'd been through? And she didn't even know it yet. Maybe Betty was mistaken. Maybe it was a ruse to get him off his ass where Grace was concerned. Would she even believe him if he told her, or would she think the baby was the only reason he wanted to be with her?

Sam shook his head and slowed to a stop. He glanced back at the hospital entrances and spun around. He'd never walk away and leave her to deal with this on her own. He'd headed back for the hospital door when he spotted Betty leaning against a post watching him. He stomped toward her.

"I've only known her a week. What the hell am I supposed to do with that information?"

"You knew the minute she entered your office." Betty rested her palm over Sam's heart. "And you know her in here."

"And Grace? If she knows that you told me about the baby, she'll think that is the only reason I'm with her."

"She's already fallen for you, Stone. So, man up."

He let her words sink in as he stepped around her and headed into the hospital.

"Second floor. Just follow the smell of coffee," she hollered out.

Sam got on the elevator and rode it up to the second floor. With each passing floor, his determination grew. He could do this. He could convince her. Sam stepped off the elevator and pulled out his phone. Ducking into one of the empty hospital rooms, he made a call to his attorney and ordered the paperwork to be ready by the time he arrived.

Sam stepped out of the room, and the aroma of coffee drifted to his nose making him smile. He turned in the same direction and followed as it got stronger. He found Grace in an alcove behind the nurses' station pouring a cup of coffee.

"I'm not sure that's good for the baby."

Grace raised her brow and slowly put the coffee pot back. She lifted the black coffee to her lips. "Good thing it's not my boobs those screamers will be dining on."

"Yet," he amended. "How are your sisters?"

"Better." Grace grinned. "The drugs kicked in, and the babies are beautiful and loud, just like their mommas." Grace set her coffee down and led him toward the nursery. "How did you know I was here?"

"I saw you leave your office with your sisters. Call it a gut feeling." He turned to look at the babies in the soundproof nursery. Baby Menzies had a head full of red hair and was swaddled in a pink blanket covered with elephants. "Wow. Quinn is going to have a handful." He glanced to the only blonde baby swaddled in a pink blanket. "Wow, they both had girls. They're both going to have their hands full."

"I know. Isn't it great?" Grace smiled and gestured to the bandage peeking out from beneath his shirt. "You look better. I'm glad you're okay."

"Not quite," he said and stepped toward her. He cupped her cheek and pressed a soft kiss to her lips. "I need your help."

"Again? So soon?" she asked, pulling his lips back to hers. She kissed him again, only this time in a proper hello-I've-missed-the-shit-out-of-you kiss.

"Yeah, I'll explain on the way, but I need you to come with me."

"Where to?" Her brows dipped.

"Answer me one thing first."

She raised her brow in question.

"Do I still give you those butterflies when you see me from across the room?"

Grace's lips twitched into a smile, but she didn't answer.

"Do you crave my touch?"

No answer, just a twinkle in her eyes.

He repeated her wish list from the first day she'd walked into his office. "I'm tall with dark hair and successful. Not to mention secure enough within myself to date an attractive, successful woman. I'm good in bed, passionate, romantic. I have a muscular body, and I'm smart. I think I qualify for your wish list."

"You left out adventurous and open-minded with my career choice."

"I think we both know that I believe in you, and I'm open to adventure."

"Your point?" she asked, as if unsure where he was headed with his questioning.

"You saved my life. You saved my brother from a loveless marriage, and his life too. You're beautiful and stunning and amazing, and I can't help you find a date. Not when I want to keep you for myself."

She smiled up at him and patted his chest. "I already told you I'd date you."

He shook his head. "It's more complicated than that."

"I don't understand," she said, dropping her hand from his chest.

He picked it back up and held it over his heart. "Do you trust me?"

"Of course." She smiled.

"Good. We have some things to iron out. Come with me."

Chapter 16

Sam kept his palm on the small of her back and led Grace into the attorney's office building.

"What are we doing here?" she whispered as they stepped into the elevator.

"Removing any doubt so you know that whatever I say is genuine," he answered.

"I don't understand. If you're here for a prenup, I think you're putting the cart way before the horse. Normally, people date before popping the question." She stepped out of the elevator onto the attorney's floor. Sam led her down the hall, and they were shown into a conference room. Sam gestured for her to sit, and she did, but he continued to stand.

"Grace. I knew the moment you walked into my office that it was going to take a special guy to make you happy, and I hope like hell that I'm the one you choose because I'll spend a lifetime trying to do just that."

"Sam. What are you talking about? I agreed we should date. Why are we here?"

Sam slid a packet in front of her and gestured for her to read. "No matter what happens, or where you and I go from here, I will always, always be there for you and our child."

"Sam, I'm not—"

"Betty thinks you are."

Grace rose from her chair and slowly backed away. "Is that why you came to find me? You think I'm carrying your baby?"

"I was coming to find you before Betty blindsided me with the fact that you might be pregnant." He gestured to the paperwork. "Those papers seal all of my involvement and promise to always be there for our child, no matter what. I don't want you to think that the baby was and is the only reason I want to be with you, because it's not. I'll love that baby, no matter what, and I'll love her mom too, regardless of whether she's just my girlfriend or agrees to be my wife."

"You've only known me a few weeks, Sam. You're talking crazy. Did you let Aunt Betty rub some of her crazy off and onto you? We haven't even had a real date."

Sam picked a pen off the table and signed the papers at the bottom. "Our unborn daughter gets everything unless we marry, and then it transfers to you. It's done."

"I don't want your stuff." He'd lost his mind.

"I was hoping you wanted me, now that you know I'm not dating you because of the pregnancy, and because I really, truly, do want to be with you, Grace. Only you."

"Think rationally, Sam. What if we don't even like each other? In a month you could be tired of me."

Sam's lips twitched into a smile. "I'll never tire of you. You make me smile; you make me laugh; you make my heart feel full, and you're the best plus-one wedding date I could have ever hoped for. We'll take it as slow as you want or as fast as you want. I could pick out a ring today, or I'll date you the way you deserve, well, minus the wine. I promise to spend the rest of my life making both of my girls happy."

"Did she say we were having a girl, because Aunt Betty is the founder of her own crazy town? She's got the fake ID to prove it. She could totally be lying to you. I wouldn't put it past her to be manipulating you."

Sam closed the distance between them and pulled Grace flush against his body. "She can't manipulate feelings I already have, and it doesn't matter what gender we have. I love you, Grace. I never thought I'd be the one to fall so hard, and so quickly, but I did. It happened. I'll win you over; you're worth the effort, even if I have to read all your books to help me convince you to be mine."

Grace grinned. "You already have. I have one condition."

"Name it."

"Vegas. No wedding, no crazy family, except for a witness. Just you and me in Vegas."

"Your jet or mine?"

The End.

Thank you all for reading my stories. I really do appreciate you! I've been playing around with an entirely new series that should be out in 2017, but not before Becca has her own highlander to contend with and boy is he something else.

Text KATE to 313131 and get a text message on release dates!

Sign up for her newsletters at www.kateallenton.com

Other Books by Kate Allenton

Suggested Reading Order
BENNETT SISTERS BOX SET (Books 1-4 in one bundle, 1218 pages)
BENNETT SISTERS BOX SET VOLUME 2 (Books 5-7 in one bundle, 517 pages}
INTUITION (Book 1)
TOUCH OF FATE (Book 2)
MIND PLAY (Book 3)
THE RECKONING (Book 4)
REDEMPTION (Book 5)
CHANCE ENCOUNTERS (Book 6)
DESTINED HEARTS (Book 7)

PHANTOM PROTECTORS BOX SET (Books 1-4 in one bundle, 964 pages)

RECKLESS ABANDON (Book 1)
BETRAYAL (Book 2)
UNTAMED (Book 3)
GUIDED LOYALTY (Book 4)

CARRINGTON-HILL INVESTIGATIONS
DECEPTION (Book 1)
DEADLY DESIRE (Book 2)

SHIFTER PARADISE BOX SET
NOT MY SHIFTER/ SINFULLY CURSED

KARMA

SOPHIE MASTERSON SERIES/ DIXON SECURITY
LIFTING THE VEIL (Book 1)
BEYOND THE VEIL (Book 2)
VEILED INTENTIONS (Book 3)
VEILED THREATS (Book 4)

THE LOVE FAMILY SERIES
SKYLAR (BOOK1)
DECLAN (BOOK 2)
FLYNN (BOOK 3)
REED (BOOK 4)
LANDON (BOOK 5)
ALEXIS (BOOK 6)
GABE (BOOK 7)
JACKSON (BOOK 8)

LINKED INC.
DEADLY INTENT (BOOK 1)

PSYCHIC LINK (BOOK 2)
PSYCHIC CHARM (BOOK 3)
PSYCHIC GAMES (BOOK 4)

HELL BOUND
MYSTIC TIDES BOX SET

KATE ALLENTON

ABOUT THE AUTHOR

Kate has lived in Florida for most of her entire life. She enjoys a quiet life with her husband and two kids.

Kate has pulled all-nighters finishing her favorite books and also writing them. She says she'll sleep when she's dead or when her muse stops singing off key.

She loves creating worlds full of suspense, secrets, hunky men, kick ass heroines, steamy sex and oh yeah the love of a lifetime. Not to mention an occasional ghost and other supernatural talents thrown into the mix.

www.ingramcontent.com/pod-product-compliance
Lightning Source LLC
Chambersburg PA
CBHW051240170626
46809CB00004B/1406